Get LENIN

by

Robert Craven

ISBN   1461194016

EAN   978-1461194019

'Get LENIN' is published by Night Publishing who can be contacted at: http://www.nightpublishing.com.

The story contains several characters well known to history, such as Adolf Hitler, Joseph Stalin, Joseph Goebbels and Heinrich Himmler. However, all the principal characters who are not well-known historical figures are fictional, and any resemblance to anyone living or dead is accidental.

To my family

Chapter 1

September 1938 – Munich

The early-hours sounds of the city drifted up through the hotel window - trams, cars and music. Spotlights fanned the still summer night, casting swooping shadows around the room.

Eva Molenaar pulled a robe about her, slipped from the bed and reached into her handbag to retrieve her cigarette case and lighter. Her head swam with vodka, but she still felt in control. Tapping the cigarette four times against the case before lighting up, she sat on the window sill and viewed Munich. Every building was draped with red swastikas, giving the street the look of a theatre proscenium.

She looked back at the Soviet Attaché snoring in the bed, his big, shaven head resembling a bulb. The Russian had been an inexhaustible seam of information. Whatever the outcome of the conference, her homeland was finished.

Her next thoughts were of her family and her handler. The cigarette case was a gift from him. It was silver, slim and anonymous.

She dressed quietly. She had been careful as to where she had put her clothes. She switched the bathroom light on and the snoring from the room beyond increased as if in response. Her hair she could do nothing about, but she made an effort to control it. Splashing cold water onto her face and applying make-up, she stepped back to review herself, turned out the light and slipped out of the room.

In the corridor raucous singing and the sound of a phonograph boomed from the suite where the Italian delegation was staying. Street girls flitted from room to room, one or two giving her a sisterly look as she passed them. At the end of the corridor, a two-man SS security detail checked her papers. At 3 a.m. and with so many girls in constant motion, they paid little heed to her, waving her through.

Eva crossed the foyer. The night-staff were so bored they didn't even look up to see a pretty girl passing them by. Journalists, writers and Pathé news teams sat smoking and drinking. Some were shouting into lobby phones to editorial departments across the world's time zones. German songs bellowed from the residents' bar.

At the second check point she came under greater scrutiny, encountering more plain clothes Gestapo. Her papers, issued via the Dutch Embassy, were gallantly handed back with a suave smile. The Fraulein should not be travelling the city at night alone – one of them strode out of the foyer onto the street and hailed a passing taxi. Eva beamed thanks to them, flashing her thigh as she slipped into the car.

As the taxi made its way through the city, an almost New Year's Eve feeling filled the night.

'What do you think of Neville Chamberlain flying in tomorrow? The eyes of the world will be on Munich!' announced the driver, cheerfully breaking the silence.

'Let's hope it's the last conference,' agreed Eva nonchalantly, making it a point to stare out of the window,

'Good for business, though!' He raised a smile but noted the pretty girl seemed lost in her thoughts. Undeterred, he kept the conversation going but ensured it was small talk. It killed the time.

Eva's German was fluent but her accent still had traces of her native Polish. She replied occasionally to the driver who was extolling the joys of the city before she interrupted him asking him to drop her off. Despite his protests, she insisted she was suffering from car sickness and would rather walk the last block to clear her head. She tipped him and waved sweetly, insisting she was ok as he sped back to the hotel.

Dawn was breaking over the skyline. A young couple passed her hand-in-hand, wishing her a good morning, the young man dressed in crisp Wehrmacht uniform, the girl in a beautiful cocktail dress, revellers from one of the many embassy balls. They both couldn't have been more than nineteen years old. As Eva stepped into the hotel where she was staying, a pair of Messerschmitt fighters tore across the dawn skyline, glinting like knives. Ascending smoothly to escort the in-coming diplomatic flights, they banked up into the vanilla coloured clouds and disappeared. The street became silent again. Eva collected her key, using the name De Witte.

In her room, Eva did one thing before retiring to bed. Opening her wardrobe, she took out her long blue raincoat. She had placed a half-full packet of cigarettes in the pocket. She took them out, intent on transferring them into the silver cigarette case. Sliding her thumbnail along the glued edge, she opened out the carton. She reached for the cigarette case. It was fitted on the inside with two strips of metal that swung out on a hinge. Each strip was fitted with buttons equidistant on both sides. Placing the carton's thin edge between the two strips of metal, she pressed them together, the points under the tab pushing out the cardboard. They were a combination of dots, visible to the eye only when angled into the light, but to her handler a simple code in fine-point Braille.

She paused before the next sequence. Should Germany invade the Soviet Union, Lenin's body would be a priority evacuation. The attaché had snorted in derision through the shot glass as he spoke those words. She input the message. Using one of her hairpins, she fastened the carton together, placing three cigarettes back. She then stowed the cigarette packet back in her coat pocket.

Removing the Braille strips, she released the hinge holding the plates together. With the Gestapo being so diligent during the conference she couldn't afford to have these strips discovered. She put one plate along the hemline of her overcoat for its return to British Intelligence and, stepping out into the corridor, she went over to the open-grilled elevator and slipped the other plate through the gap between the lift door and the floor. It dropped from sight without a sound.

She lay on the bed, pulled the top cover around her, and replayed the banquet where she had met the Russian.

The first recollection was of the room filled with the smell of pomade, cigars and aftershave. She had committed to memory the faces and names around her to the medley the orchestra was playing - Oswald and Diana Mosley, Unity Mitford, Von Ribbentrop,

Molotov, Daladier, and a tall American businessman named Donald T Kincaid. She had met dozens of his ilk in her time and this one was no different. He was about fifty, rich in a vulgar fashion and accompanied by a young platinum blonde. He regarded Eva and most of her Eastern European counterparts with barely disguised contempt. Still, he had leered at her through the thick lenses of his glasses whenever the blonde he was escorting was engaged elsewhere in conversation.

Eva spotted the Russian Attaché in an ill-fitting uniform from the photograph memorised earlier. He was looking at her as she had hoped, his small eyes glinting with lust. Breaking from a group of publishers and freelance reporters, she struck up a conversation in Russian. In no time he had moved past clumsy flirting to doe-eyed adoration. Closing her eyes, she shuddered for what might happen during the remainder of the evening, but in fact nothing did as the drunken Russian passed out struggling to get his boots off.

Kincaid made her nervous, though. With his sort of money she would be easy to find should he decide to take up the chase. On several occasions he had jettisoned the blonde to make small talk, ignoring the Russian's ire.

* * *

The dawn light glinting through the heavy curtains woke her. It was 8am. Eva showered quickly, slipped into a formal skirt and jacket, and took out her perfume. Spraying some into the air, she

9

stepped into the fine mist and out again. She took the overcoat from the wardrobe and spilled the remainder of the perfume onto it. Draping it over her arm, she took the stairs down to the lobby where she singled out a waitress serving coffee to some English journalists looking lost amid their luggage. The waitress was thin and angular-faced, with her fair hair pulled back severely.

'Pardon me, Fraulein, could you ensure this is cleaned? I must leave for Stuttgart this afternoon.' Touching the waitress on the arm with a pre-arranged signal, she handed her the coat.

Eva smiled faux-shyly at the journalists, apologising for the interruption. The waitress smiled back, giving a slight nod in recognition of the signal and of the codeword 'Stuttgart'. She told Eva that it would take an hour to clean and directed her to the breakfast room.

Eva took a seat furthest from the door and ordered a coffee and pastry from a gaunt-looking waiter. Lighting a cigarette, she exhaled slowly as she glanced around the room. Satisfied no-one was paying attention to her, she began to relax.

A group of Americans commandeered the table beside her, their banter and relaxed manner adding to the ambience. They all appeared well-groomed and well-dressed, unlike their British counterparts in the foyer outside. Two smiled over at her, inviting her to join them. She demurred with a smile.

'Can't wait to hear what these guys have to say,' said the one with leading man looks. He lit up a pipe, drawing on it in measured puffs.

'We're after all talking about a bunch of book burners and their appeasers,' agreed his companion. His eyes kept drifting over to Eva as he spoke. Like his friend, he was handsome and appeared erudite.

'Editorial's gonna have a field day. I wonder if they still burn books over here.' The conversation stopped once their orders arrived accompanied by a large pot of coffee.

The waitress who had taken Eva's coat came into the restaurant looking for her. When she spotted her, she came over and offered her a newspaper to read. Eva thanked her with a smile and, after skimming the pages, found the crossword. Reaching into her bag she withdrew a pen and began to fill in the clues with coded messages. She folded the paper into her bag and prepared to hand it back to the waitress when her coat was ready.

All around her was laughter, the clatter of cutlery and the German waitresses flirting with the Americans. It almost seemed the human species was staring into annihilation and keen to breed as compensation.

The coffee arrived and Eva noted how bad the waiter's skin was. She summoned a smile to thank him, hoping it wouldn't encourage him to hover.

The coffee was fresh and strong. Her hangover was abating and the pastry was warm from the kitchen. Now all she had to do for the next two hours was stay alive, her thoughts drifting with the cigarette smoke.

Do they still burn books over here?

Chapter 2

May 10th 1933 - Berlin

The ceremonial pyre raged on the Opernplatz, sending sparks and ashes into the cooling twilight, captured on film by the Ministry or Propaganda. Encircling it, a cordon of Ernst Rohm's SA stood holding flambeaus in rigid attention. Curious onlookers watched as the books were hurled into the flames, fluttering upwards like broken doves before falling into the inferno. Nationalistic songs were shouted with gusto by the SA and Hitler Youth, followed by fire-oath chants with straight-arm salutes as the fire was fed.

Across Weimar Germany this scene was repeating itself, the nation's intelligentsia being singled out for 'enlightenment' in National Socialism by Adolf Hitler and Joseph Goebbels. Manuscripts, paintings and etchings marked as 'un-German' were being incinerated in an orgy of destruction. Student leaders wearing swastika armbands directed more groups of SA to rooms and lecture halls that had been under surveillance for months. The libraries were stripped of their contents and precious tomes were earmarked for destruction in a clinical manner, impelled by the day long radio broadcasts and posters plastered up all over the city.

Across from the platz where the inferno raged, in the basement theatre space of Humboldt University, Eva Molenaar put her dog-eared script down. She could hear the roar of the crowd drifting into the room. In the small rehearsal space she stood with her fiancé and fellow actor, Jonas Zamoyski, and the director, Herr Gruber.

'I hear they're burning books by Jack London and H.G. Wells,' she said uneasily.

'And Thomas Mann,' added Jonas, glancing toward the door. Another roar from the platz drifted in and the chants seemed to come in waves.

Instinctively she moved closer to Jonas. Gruber leaned toward them. 'It seems wolves and Martians have unsettled Doctor Goebbels. Now pay attention you two. Ignore those pyromaniacs and their goons over at the platz.'

Eva noted the script was shaking slightly in the director's hands. The noise outside swelled momentarily. Gruber glanced up toward the door, then turned to the couple, clearing his throat quietly. 'They are in love, yes, your characters?'

Eva and Jonas exchanged a glance. Jonas' eyes twinkled and Eva dimpled back. They nodded. With a gesture, Gruber had Eva sitting on the edge of the bed and moved Jonas upstage, then stepped back. Satisfied with their positioning, he continued, 'Now think, what would they be doing? It's the morning. This scene, Jonas, is like Romeo and Juliet, Act 3, Scene 3. The lovers are about to part after their first night together; the sowing of the first doubts, of love and loss. He's leaving her chamber as they talk. What action could he be doing?' Gruber was inspired, moving around in his out-sized suit. He looks wonderfully crumpled, thought Eva.

'Getting dressed,' grinned Jonas, tipping a wink to her.

'Excellent. Yes! Getting dressed.'

Eva blushed deeply. Gruber noted it swept down to her collar bone. Gruber clapped his hands. 'Now again!'

They were preparing a short two-hander that Jonas had written and performed with Eva at Warsaw's summer theatre. As a result they both had been invited to Berlin to perform for the student body studying Polish drama, notably the works of Leon Schiller. Herr Gruber, a disciple of Brecht, wanted to add a more nihilistic slant to the work. They were discussing the piece further when the door to the rehearsal room was kicked in.

Two SA troopers in their late-teens stood red-faced, sweating drunk, with batons in their hands.

Gruber strode forward, demanding the reason for the intrusion. He was beaten repeatedly then stamped on. He fell to the ground. Eva screamed. Jonas placed himself in front of her as the two SA troopers strutted in. They ignored Jonas' shouts of protest as they were drawn to the beautiful young girl. No more than seventeen, her auburn hair sat shoulder-length, framing a heart-shaped face and grey Nordic eyes.

'Well, well, well what do we have here?' the taller of the two troopers said, ogling Eva. The smaller one with porcine eyes snatched away her script.

'A play is it?' he slurred, looking back at Gruber's body. Gruber lay still with blood now pooling around him. The trooper tried to read the print. When he couldn't, he proceeded to tear the script slowly and deliberately.

'Looks like degenerate Jewish literature,' he sneered.

'Wir sind nicht jüdisch,' countered Jonas slowly.

'Any nudity?' rasped the other one, his eyes never leaving Eva.

Eva drew closer to Jonas. Her mind was frozen in terror. The two Brownshirts moved in and out of the minimal overhead lighting. The smell of smoke, sweat and Scotch whisky assailed her. One of them unsheathed a knife from his jack boot and sidled toward her, grinning.

'Yep, nudity alright.'

Jonas lunged at him. 'Run!' he shouted at Eva.

She bolted for the door as the three men struggled. The smaller one grabbed her by her hair, pulling a clump of it out. Leaping over Gruber's prone body, her forward momentum drove her into the corridor. Her neck was wet and she was bleeding. Pressing the palm of her hand against the wound, she sprinted for the courtyard.

Jonas floored the first attacker with a punch to the jaw. The smaller one ducked under the follow through and slashed him across the arm with his knife. The blade cut deep into the muscles of Jonas' forearm. With his free hand he smacked the man down onto the floor, the knife clattering away from them. Bleeding heavily, Jonas bolted for the door.

He paused deliberately to lure the men away from Eva, hoping their bloodlust was sated and they would ignore her. Their stumbling footfalls and whooping cat-calls told him they were behind him. Pausing for another beat, he watched Eva running for the courtyard. He spied a stairwell to the upper corridors and bounded up the steps two at a time, his wound leaving a spotted trail.

Eva sprinted toward the university's square. In it stood two furniture removal vans with their engines idling, the back doors open. A line of SA and Nazi sympathisers were loading hundreds of books onto them. They were surrounded by angry students and lecturers pushing, shoving and throwing punches. The SA in turn retaliated with batons and kicks. More SA arrived in trucks. The campus was fast becoming a battlefield.

A disturbance overhead made Eva look up. She screamed.

Jonas was pitched over the third floor balcony onto the cobbles below by the two troopers, where he was set upon by more SA, throwing books aside and sprinting over to him. They started stamping, kicking and swinging their batons onto his unprotected head.

Eva tried to run to him. Ellen Eidelstein, a girl Eva and Jonas had been rooming with, ran toward her from the student protest around the van.

Eva was shrieking and struggling to get to Jonas. Ellen pulled her away, removing her scarf and putting it over Eva's head in case her attackers could see her below. The two men on the balcony were scanning the square, their faces contorted in a drunken rage. Ellen dragged Eva into the mass of protesting students who started running after the vans toward the inferno. The two women ran past it into the unforgiving night filled with the songs of German might and the fluttering ashes of literature.

After an hour of skirting side streets and avoiding crowds, they made it back to Ellen's modest student digs under the cover of night. Sleep wouldn't come. Eva rocked in the bed as Ellen hugged her and tried to soothe her. Eva sat up rigid and stared, the light through the window framing her in stark light; her eye sockets pitch black like a skull.

Next morning, after the mob had dispersed, Ellen went back to the university to try to collect Eva's belongings. Mindful of her own striking Semitic looks, she bundled herself into bulky clothes and covered her lush black hair with a plain brown scarf.

In the dressing room behind the rehearsal space, Ellen found only detritus. The stage's scenery was smashed to matchwood and strewn across the room as if struck by a hurricane.

Gruber's body was missing, but a thick trail of blood disappeared into the corridor. She found Eva's suitcase. It smelled of urine. Her underclothes were scattered and her make-up bag had been emptied. Ellen picked around and uncovered in a corner Eva's passport and identity papers, miraculously preserved amid the ashes of a fire. The faint whiff of Scotch came off the remains. Whoever had lit it had left in a hurry, perhaps disturbed.

Ellen started to weep silently. The once beautiful city of Berlin was now at the mercy of the mob. Pulling herself together, she made her way through the corridors, out into the shadows of the cloisters and slipped out onto the main street.

'We have to find Jonas, Eva. We have to try to find out if he's alive or dead,' she had whispered over and over, trying to drown out the whispered cries from Eva's lips that evening.

17

After an immense effort, Ellen and Eva, swaddled and holding each other like two old ladies, began the painful search for Jonas. For Eva the journey was a series of indelible images - trams, hospital walls, morgues, unsympathetic staff and hostile police. Her beauty, even in grief, received unwelcome attention from the police and SA patrols that were gathering in strength nearly every day on the street. Every morgue they visited smelled like a butcher's shop.

She remembered Ellen shouting at a nurse who told her to her face she wouldn't talk to a Jew.

Eventually they found Jonas in the morgue of the Charite Horsaal. They walked with an attendant amid gurneys with sheets draped over them. Spotting them, the attendant had put down his mop and offered to help. Eva watched him, hunched and old. He was sympathetic and listened to their enquiry with deep-brown concerned eyes. She described Jonas. When the attendant asked for some identifying feature, her mind froze momentarily. Then she spotted a hand sticking out from under a sheet with a ring she recognised. The ring, with an agate stone fashioned to an oval, was a gift for his twentieth birthday from her. She had bought it for him in the market square in the shadow of St Mary's Basilica in Krakow. A bloodied stump at the middle phalanx of his middle finger indicated his finger had been cut in an attempt to remove it. The morgue attendant pulled the sheet back. The face and body of her dead lover brought a hideous scream from Eva as she tried with her hands to block the bloodied, crushed visage. None of his features remained intact. The face was swollen, flattened and purple. The once-lush flaxen hair was matted brown with blood. The beautiful mouth that she had kissed a thousand times was torn, split and discoloured. Ellen held her close as Eva's body, racked with spasms, screamed out his name, her voice echoing out into the corridor.

Ellen left, telling Eva to remain there as she went to find a local undertaker.

Eva took the mutilated hand with the agate ring and held it. She summoned every prayer she knew, believing somehow that he was still alive. Despite her beseeching to Almighty God, Jonas' chest wouldn't rise. She hunted in her pockets and found a used handkerchief. She gently wiped the congealed blood from his shattered visage, her tears falling onto his face. They mixed with the blood and dirt, and clean smears of grey coloured skin appeared as she wiped him tenderly.

By chance Ellen had found an undertaker in the hospital foyer, a kindly man named Bergen. Rohm's thugs had had a busy night; Bergen was collecting the remains of two men beaten to death on the street by the SA. Bergen and Ellen returned to the morgue to find Eva keening gently into Jonas' ear as she cleaned him tenderly.

Eva accompanied Jonas' remains back to Krakow to his family after telegraphing them the dreadful news. She pawned her diamond engagement ring as a down-payment for the coffin, storage and transport of Jonas' body. She met his parents at the border station with Bergen. The coffin was removed from the hearse and placed on board. The family greeted her coldly, believing that Eva was somehow responsible for Jonas' fate.

'This pretty and flirty girl took my son to Berlin and brought this horror upon us,' cried his mother, Zoya, at the sight of the coffin.

Eva bade farewell to Ellen at the station, promising to stay in touch, neither one really believing it through their tears.

The journey by train was fraught. Eva tried to comfort Zoya who scowled at her beneath the black shawl. The family whispered among themselves, throwing glances in her direction, offering no comfort. Jonas' father, Christian Zamoyski, who had connections in the government, had contacted the German embassy to lodge an official protest. His enquiries, along with the Polish Embassy's demand for an explanation, were ignored.

Two days later, Jonas was buried in the family plot, his parents, four brothers and three sisters weeping under the gently falling rain. Eva's parents were buried here in this cemetery too, killed in a car crash a year earlier. She was once told that no two Polish gravestones are ever alike and, looking across the graveyard, Eva couldn't see a single matching silhouette. She stood by their graveside amid six uneven lines of private proud headstones, back from Jonas' grave. Her Grandmother Agnieszka stood with her, weeping silently. Her Grandfather Henk stood with the grieving family.

The next day, Eva was summoned to Jonas' family home, a comfortable middle-class dwelling that to Eva had been always filled with laughter. As she stepped over the threshold she felt the pall that had descended throughout the house.

Christian Zamoyski seemed to almost look through her as he held his arm out before her. 'Good afternoon, Eva. Please step into my study,'

The room was dimly lit. Somewhere in a room above a woman was keening. Occasional sounds rang out, followed by cries. Christian had somehow shrunk in stature. An ill-fitting jacket seemed to flap about him on a hidden breeze. With a sigh he slumped into the chair behind a large desk and from a drawer he produced a cheque book. He scratched across it with a pen to the slow tick of the grandfather clock in the gloom. 'Thank you for bringing him safely to the border, Eva.' He handed her the cheque. It was twice the value of her engagement ring.

'Thank you, Mr. Zamoyski,' she stammered with tears pinching the corners of her eyelids, 'this is too much.'

'The family are waiting for you in the kitchen,' Christian whispered as he rose unsteadily. Sighing deeply, he seemed to lose some more of his body mass as he walked toward the door. He guided her through the hall, past the staircase where she and Jonas had chased each other as children, past the cellar door where they had enjoyed their first kiss, and into the kitchen.

Zoya sat motionless at the table. Behind her, standing in rigid attention, was the family. Her voice broke several times and rose in register as she spoke to Eva. 'You are never to call, never to visit the grave, never to contact us for any reason again. Never, ever again.' Jonas' brothers and sisters all stood stone-faced and unresponsive to Eva's pleas.

'Vidma!' hissed Zoya, crossing herself three times, her rosary

21

beads rattling in her thin white fist, her ferocity silencing Eva.

Eva left the house, her world spinning. These people, who had welcomed her, now sent her away vilified. She was an outcast from the family that had adopted her since she was thirteen. *Vidma*, a witch - that wounded her deeply.

She returned to her grandparents' house on the outskirts of the city. Henk stood at the doorway and held her close as she wept. This was now the third tragedy within a year: Henk and Aga losing a son, then a daughter-in-law, and now Jonas, the bright lad who dreamed of being an actor. It was almost too much for the three of them to bear.

Something became numb, dead and lifeless inside Eva. All she could see was a creeping darkness. It started at the edges of her vision, peripheral shadows drawing in closer like curtains. She thought at first it was a trick of the light as she brushed her hair first thing in the morning. The mirror on her dresser seemed to have developed a smoky frame.

Her weight dropped and Grandmother Aga fretted. 'Eat, child, eat,' she'd whisper into her ear as she placed warm soup and bread on the table, tutting quietly later as she'd take back the untouched food while maintaining a silent perseverance. Any morsel consumed was viewed as a victory.

Before his retirement Henk had lectured English and Classic Philosophy at the Jan Matejko Academy in Krakow. He managed to secure a librarian's assistant position for Eva there.

Amid the Trappist-quiet halls, Eva began her gradual

recuperation. She hid amid shapeless clothes and a plain brown head scarf. She never made eye contact. She sought sanctuary in the library's books. Drawn to languages, she immersed herself in books alone in her bedroom at night. Henk and Aga began to help her, his natural ear for language beginning to build a bridge to his broken granddaughter. Aga's German, stilted and guttural, gave Eva a feel for a language. She could sometimes guess ahead of her grandmother what the next sentence was going to be.

For the first time in her life she entered her grandfather's library, to her simply a vast oaken door secured by a Gothic black lock while she was growing up. Beyond the door stood high bookcases, beautifully fashioned in mahogany, containing wall-to-wall leather-bound volumes accessed with the help of a sliding ladder.

Henk touched her shoulder, the reassurance and strength flowing from his digits into her soul. 'Stay in here as long as you want, Eva.' His voice was gentle and mellow, his Polish still carrying a Dutch cadence. It had made her laugh as a child. She loved its sound; it reminded her somehow of treacle.

She whiled away the autumn and winter months there. Henk procured a large well-worn leather armchair for her to coil up in. She read by the firelight. Aga would leave food and tea for her, stepping in quietly and touching Eva's arm gently, as silent as a ghost.

Henk moved in the piano, a family heirloom, upright and ornately inlaid with delicate flowers, and Eva discovered old studies she'd learned as a child. All the manuscripts of sheet music Eva uncovered were dusted down for her. Sitting at the stool, she set the old wooden metronome and began to learn how to play again. She would lose herself for hours in the music of Johan Sebastian Bach, beginning with the Anna Magdalena notebook.

Slowly as a flower buds, Eva's soul began to heal.

* * *

The following spring semester brought Theo Kassinski. He was tall and lean. Dark curls flowed around his handsome features and he had an innate assurance of his place in the world. He was an unkempt, handsome artist with a smile for her every time he came up to borrow a book. He was looking for a model to draw and he guessed correctly that under her shapeless clothes Eva was a goddess. He asked her to model for him, assuring her he wasn't interested in her other than her being his contract model. At the desk he had scratched out a quick pencil sketch of her to prove that he could draw. She merely glanced at the sketch - it didn't move her in any particular way - and agreed with the briefest of nods. On the back of the page he wrote out the address of his studio and handed it to her.

That Saturday she went to the address. The studio, a reconditioned garret above a warehouse, contained a cold water sink, a brass bed and basic kitchenette. Trestle tables lined the far wall with the paraphernalia of his vocation. The room had a co-ordinated chaos about it, where food, drink and clothing lay piled amid oils, canvas, brushes, reams of paper and sheets of hardboard.

A screen covered an ornate ancient commode, though rarely as their relationship developed did they avail themselves of it, preferring to take a break at the small café across the road, Theo more often than not dappled from head to toe in paint.

She disrobed in the spring sunshine in his studio, moving in poses as Theo sketched her quickly. Both subject and artist took a dispassionate view of each other, and yet Eva found herself every weekend in the studio. They were alone for hours on end, the scratching of pencil, charcoals and pastels marked by the passage of the sun across the wooden floor, the easel a barrier between them.

She allowed her mind to close. Every breath was measured, timed - sometimes short, other times for as long as her lungs would allow. She started to push the limits of her body, twisting herself into complex poses, this breathing exercise making her focus her concentration on the pose relishing, the challenge it presented. A subtle chemistry developed between them where she could almost guess what he was going to ask next. At the end of each session, he would proudly display his renderings as he turned the easel around to her.

For Theo, this arrangement was perfect. Eva never uttered a word, nor sighed, nor complained about having to stand still. He was a rich, bored scion of a local clothing factory owner, though he showed real potential according to some of the gallery owners he had shown his work to. He was Jewish, and always at odds with his father for not attending synagogue and eschewing his heritage and studies. They didn't square with his chosen nihilistic existence. He would tell her this from behind the easel, usually when he was struggling with his materials. It eased the tension within him. Other than his clashes with his father, she learned he was an only child like her and devoted to his mother.

The months drifted slowly and she watched herself appear more life-like as Theo developed and honed his skills on paper and canvas. Crude charcoal outlines disappeared; shadowing and light became more subtle until he produced a piece unlike anything else he had done.

He had captured her perfectly; Eva was lying naked on the floor, her legs together twisting away from her torso, one arm draped across her breasts, the other arm behind her, spilling lush auburn tresses. It was if she was caught in mid-leap across the sugar paper. He had fashioned a smile on her features, telling her that when she did so, which was rarely, she was a radiant. He opened a bottle of wine and, for the first time in a year, she smiled briefly and Theo was duly mesmerised.

On an impulse, she accompanied him to his bed at the rear of the studio as he took her hand, but the dark edges still hung about her peripheral vision despite his gentle attentive efforts.

'You know, Eva,' he said, an ashtray resting on his chest as they shared a cigarette in the tiny metal bed, 'you should try for the movies. They have a film unit in the university. They're always looking for actors and actresses.'

She exhaled with one eyebrow raised and a sceptical moue. Smiling, he swept his hand around the room. Eva hadn't looked around it much. Across every wall pictures of her were pinned up - nude, clothed, sitting, lying, posing, and head and shoulder portrait studies. In every one of them her eyes had a haunted quality, the last and most beautiful image of her at her most wistful.

He stubbed out his cigarette and rose to dress,

'With your grace, beauty and theatrical training, Eva, it'd be academic you'd have no problems being accepted. I know some of the film students; I could introduce you.'

Chapter 3

That summer she travelled to Paris with Theo and Dariusz Spzilman, a film student that he shared digs with. 1930s Paris was a Mecca for Theo, the epitome of art and beauty, for Dariusz, the centre of film.

Theo's French was rudimentary and Dariusz's non-existent. They needed a translator and Eva agreed to accompany them. They took a two-bed cold water apartment in La Pigalle, Eva with a room to herself, the men sharing a room with two single beds. Her room was more of a corner garret, cramped and warm, the bed a recovered hospital cot, robust and basic. The wardrobe contained a few new dresses and her prized blue raincoat Henk and Aga had bought for her before her departure. All three would swim in the nearby public pool every day to perform their ablutions. Theo, armed with his notebooks and charcoals, managed to persuade most of the men to allow him to sketch them while drying themselves, some taking the sketch in exchange for a cigarette, but never for cash, at his insistence.

One late summer afternoon, Theo and Dariusz posed theatrically at the top of the Eiffel Tower as they pointed out landmarks over the shimmering roofs of Paris, the wind catching their hats. Eva, snatching Dariusz's precious camera, squeezed off a shot of the men. It developed perfectly and she pinned it to the cracked and faded mirror on her battered dresser in her room. The other pictures, now creased and faded, were of Henk and Aga, and of her deceased parents, Maria and Pytoir, with Eva as a grim-faced toddler. Below them was a picture of a smiling Jonas. Every morning when applying her make-up, she would touch the photograph tenderly and reminisce.

Eva's idea of heaven was getting lost in the numerous bookstores around the city, wrapped in her trusty blue raincoat, when the men were off drinking. Theo, walking in the footsteps of his hero Toulouse Lautrec, would frequent the bordellos, restaurants and his drinking haunts that peppered the city.

By night they would gather at the Café Procope on Rue Buci with their French counterparts, the hours spent discussing cinema, philosophy and politics over simple food and carafes of wine. Eva had to grasp the language quickly as the debates got heated and found she could, becoming more often than not the referee.

Theo, perhaps caught up in the zeitgeist, announced he was a Communist, content with his bohemian lot and, as a reflection, his art became more de-structured and free-flowing. He stopped using colour, developing a tonal two and three tone style. Refusing to purchase picture frames, he set up a scrap wood stall along the Pont Notre-Dame with the sketches pinned and fluttering in the breeze.

He squandered his allowance from his father in reckless abandon. Purchasing a bicycle, he travelled around the city, his long thin legs pumping the pedals in determination, his free arm clutching his materials. For her birthday he bought Eva a camera, a simple box brownie, and she thrived on travelling around the city alone by foot, bus and metro, capturing it. Dariusz had built a dark room in the apartment and he allowed her time to learn how to develop pictures in between his projects. Theo had paid for all of the wood from his father's allowance, helping Dariusz to haul the lumber up the flights of rickety stairs and hammering the whole thing together. The apartment's window remained open most of the time after that owing to the smell of the processing chemicals.

Eva's wanderings gave her a new fulfilment, making her aware of not only her own beauty but the beauty of the city and its people. She would buy all her of dresses from the flea markets and slowly she began to eat again, filling out and regaining her superb figure. The summer nights were balmy and the bright lights of the city somehow soothing. She truly loved Paris, loved being anonymous amid its streets. Theo would smile appreciatively, charcoal poised over paper as she undressed when Dariusz was out of the apartment haunting a cinema somewhere.

Theo would sit at the cafés sketching the passing population, waiters, waitresses and patrons. Among his drawings was a quick free-flowing sketch of Samuel Beckett who one evening sat and discussed the films and style of Sergi Eisenstein with the group. Eva's English helped the Pole expand on his theories with the Irishman despite the time lag between the effusive Dariusz and the measured responses of Beckett. With Theo's quick execution, Beckett appeared all twisted and bent like a crow dashing across the page. He told them he'd be back, but was departing for Germany to report on the rise and the abuses that the new Reich was perpetrating. Kissing Eva's hand gallantly, Beckett asked her to visit Ireland sometime. Smiling back warmly, she promised she would.

Eva loved to photograph the twilight, a time of the day when the darkness around her vision seemed the most bearable, where the shadows blended rather than clashed with the available light. Beside Daruisz's reels of film, hung Eva's first images of the city; the carousels of Sacré Coeur, the city's bridges, and the museums, all captured in a moment in black and white. Sometimes she would photograph an empty street, or a square just after a rain shower. She captured the storefront lights glistening on the ground, reflected back on the puddles. She photographed the mausoleums of Père Lachaise, wandering amid the graves allowing her thoughts to drift firstly to her parents, then to her happy childhood, and then to Jonas. When alone, she believed Jonas was near, his presence almost within touching distance, a finger-tip away. The feeling would go as quickly as it had appeared, but while it was there she felt his presence as a guardian angel.

Eva began to pin her photographs around the apartment using them to cover damp patches or unsightly stains. Both Dariusz and Theo agreed she had a good eye for a picture. Her favourite image was of a mature Madame who ran a local bordello, Yvette.

Eva had struck up a conversation with her one night in a café in Montmartre. She had an iron frailty about her that drew Eva. Yvette was buxom, with lush black hair pinned up as best as the pins could do, and modestly attired in tasteful shades of purple and black. Her eyes were green and knowing. She warmed to Eva immediately and

31

agreed to be photographed. The photograph showed Yvette sitting at a table in a café looking out onto the street, a cigarette in an ashtray and a half empty coffee cup before her. Somehow Eva had caught the vibrant light in her green eyes as she smiled.

She introduced Eva to absinthe. Sometimes when alone with the photograph of Jonas, Eva drank it to numb herself when the memories of his death overwhelmed her.

Sometimes Madame Yvette would join the discussion group as they smoked and drank, open about her profession and taking Eva under her wing. She watched Eva and the almost chemical effect she had on men. The raucous debates that took place were mostly about their simply trying to impress her. Yvette wondered why Eva wasn't harnessing this power and using it to her ends,

'In this life, Eva, our youth, beauty and intelligence are sometimes all we have. In this world, men may make all the decisions, yet we have to bend them to our will. We only have so long before our bloom begins to fade and their attention starts to wander,'

Eva would learn in time to take this advice on board. Yvette had a rare quality. She genuinely liked and understood men and loved being a woman. She had a lover, a married man, and she was content to exist in the shadows. She was also discreet; her lover was a high ranking official in the government and was inclined to talk about what he did just to impress her. It was a useful power to have, she told Eva,

'Men! Their flies and their mouths they never keep closed in the presence of beauty. Use it Eva, and if they get too rough . . .' Yvette produced a small wicked mother-of-pearl handle stiletto from her boot, 'cut them.'

Theo, Eva, Dariusz and the students immersed themselves in the Paris film scene, spending long stretches in the cinemas sipping from hidden flasks of brandy and whiskey. This was followed by meals, wine and debates into the early hours. Eva and Yvette began to appear in Dariusz's projects. Devising the scene, he would produce a measuring tape and measure out the distance between the camera and subject. He would spend hours adjusting the lights borrowed from a small amateur theatre nearby to create the mood required. Returning each time to his camera perched on its tripod and peering into the viewfinder, he would grunt or laugh depending on his mood. Everything about Dariusz was measured, carefully thought out and purposely executed. In some instances a three-minute short would take three days to film at eight hour stretches.

During these long spells, Yvette would tell Eva about her life and her adventures, occasionally returning to her bordello to ensure everything was running like clockwork. Once Dariusz was satisfied with everything required for the scene, he would shout 'Action!' and Eva and Yvette would perform his carefully composed script. Then he would shoot footage of other things - animals, cars, trains, close-ups of a facial feature, random objects - and splice the various reels together, disappearing for days in his darkroom. In the student cinemas around the city, he would run his final pieces and then the whole ensemble would discuss their merits or flaws.

Theo and Dariusz took French lovers, drawing and filming them, moving onto the next one once the initial passion burned out. They told Eva they were living for the moment, without regret, without worry, never thinking of tomorrow; enjoying now. Eva found their hedonism amusing, as even when seducing women they were still competing against each other, trying to get the upper hand.

Theo would show Eva the charcoal drawings of the girls he was involved with, looking for a reaction. She would simply smile or shrug indifferently, remarking whether or not the piece was simply good or bad. This would irk him and he'd put the piece away with a grunt, making Eva smile to herself. Occasionally they would sleep together in a familiar companionable intimacy when the brandy or absinthe took hold.

During the summer, they took the train to Marseilles, the Mediterranean weather turning their skins brown. Theo had acquired a straw panama hat; Dariusz, aware of the bald patch evolving at the back of his head, wore a felt trilby. He would sit at the coffee houses with the North African aromas drifting over him, sweating, reading or writing in a white vest, his trilby tilted against the sun.

They stayed in a run-down but clean hotel managed by an Arab who would bow every time Theo and Eva passed the front desk. As in Paris, Eva had a room to herself, the men sharing the room beside her. Her room had a view of the harbour from the balcony and she woke to the sounds of the fishermen from the wharves and the cries of the gulls.

By day she would wander the narrow streets and photograph the old women, the boys kicking footballs, and the men gathered around hookahs smoking. She would sit and talk with them. As a mark of respect, she wore modest attire, a scarf or hat covering her hair, remembering her grandfather's travel journals from Iran, Egypt and Palestine.

One afternoon in her room Theo asked her to take a photograph of him; an unusual request,

'I'm thinking about going to Albi for a few days. The cathedral is supposed to have vivid depictions of the damned around its altar.' Theo noted that Eva was still concentrating on her view finder.

'What about your moody friend Sandrine?' Eva suggested without looking up.

Theo's smiled broadened. Sandrine was a waitress he had met in the Bistro Benoît and had taken as a lover. She was an unpublished poet, voluptuous with lush red hair and chestnut brown eyes. At the very mention of her name, Eva would mimic the hand gestures Sandrine would make when emphasising a point.

"She's finishing a collection of verse, cannot be disturbed.'

It was Eva's turn to smile. 'She's always finishing a collection, Theo. Still she suits you. She's passionate about what she does and very much in love with you.' The last three words were an imitation of Sandrine's voice.

Theo had hit a nerve. He liked that. 'But she's not you.' Theo had shifted his body slightly in the chair, leaning toward her. 'Noticed me all of a sudden, Kassinski?'

'Always have.' Eva looked up and met his gaze. He was handsome, unpredictable and generous, but couldn't replace Jonas, never in a lifetime. 'I'm happy with the way things are, Theo. You know the story.'

A shadow flashed across his features. 'You've never told me once how you feel about me.' He was gazing out of the window again. She felt a seismic shift in their relationship. Bringing her gaze back to the viewfinder, she said as gently as possible 'I'm still here, aren't I?'

Without looking toward her Theo said, 'Eva, I'm in love with you.' This was met with silence, followed by the shutter click.

He wouldn't make eye contact as he lit another cigarette. A shadow crossed his features as he exhaled.

Then events across the border with Spain became the centre of discussion; the gathering clouds of civil war. Theo had gone to the city of Albi to sit in the cafés of Toulouse Lautrec, armed with his sketchbooks, leaving Dariusz and Eva alone. Dariusz had told her over coffee in the men's apartment that he was in love with her. She smiled and told him also that there was no possibility it could ever be reciprocated. She told him about Jonas, that Theo was comfortable with the arrangement, and that was the way she wanted things to remain.

Though he smiled, Eva could sense a deeper hurt from him, his large eyes welling up before she looked away. On his return, Theo sensed immediately the uneasy atmosphere between Eva and Dariusz which was now hanging about them. Neither of them said anything to Theo, but he figured it was Eva's allure and a curt rejection to an advance that was the reason.

Dariusz was perhaps a little more fragile than Theo, always a bit more sensitive to criticism, whereas Theo believed absolutely in his own capabilities. The three began to drift apart over the remaining weeks.

They returned to Paris after a month, with the news that the Spanish Civil War had escalated and now the International Brigades were being formed. Dariusz and some of his French friends had signed up to fight Franco's forces. Theo and Eva tried to talk him out of it, but nothing could shake him, Eva suspecting that it was in reaction to her rejection.

'Europe's being twisted in the hands of Hitler and Mussolini's Fascism. It has to be fought,' Dariusz argued. 'The battle against this rise of evil is going to be on Spanish soil. Something has to stop the Fascists. The Socialists have to unite!'

In his fervour, almost overnight Daruisz turned his back on film. Theo and Eva were shaken by his sudden change. He hardly spoke to them from then on and left that autumn, marching over the Pyrenees and into Spain, armed with his camera, tripod, notebooks, and tilted trilby. There he and his French comrades linked up with the German, British, Irish, Canadian and German Socialists who had arrived to assist their brethren in Spain.

Theo became disillusioned and restless in Paris. Then he received the news that his father had suffered a stroke and his mother was unable to cope with him alone. He decided to return to Poland.

By the late summer of 1936, Eva found herself back in Krakow, Theo almost a distant memory; a chapter closed. He tried a few times to rekindle their relationship but his letters remained unopened. He came to the library where she had resumed her assistant duties, this time without any headscarf or over-sized clothing. She had started to radiate a confidence that attracted men and women to her, to build friendships and to socialise.

When she saw Theo with his hair trimmed, a well-cut suit and clean shaven appearance, she rejected him outright, furious at what he had become. With heated whispers across the desk, she repeated to him that they had no possible future together. It had been fun, a wonderful adventure, and she thanked him sincerely for his help in healing her. but that was it.

He scowled, his face a sneer beneath his flawless grooming, and told her it would be the last time she would ever see him. Her parting image of a man she had spent nearly two years with was of an immaculately clad businessman storming away from the desk.

She returned to her chair in Henk's library and felt the comfort of home, but couldn't settle, the fifteen months in France embedded into the marrow of her bones.

The winter turned to spring and the days began to slowly lengthen. For Christmas, Henk bought her a bicycle. She kept busy taking photographs around the country, and cycling to the central train station, travelling by train on the weekends. She would display her photographs in the library and her work came to the attention of the dramatic society. She photographed the stills for the Dramatic Society's productions and took head shots for the budding actresses who would post them hopefully out to Hollywood.

In Warsaw, one afternoon in Księgarnia Polska bookstore, she ran into Dariusz. Between the aisles of antique books and prints he walked straight up to her. It took her a split second to recognise him. He smiled, but without the usual bonhomie. His eyes had a more serious heavy-lidded appearance. His beloved trilby looked reconditioned and, to her shock, where his left arm should have been, the sleeve was pinned to the coat.

He looked down at the empty sleeve with a rueful smile. 'Lost it in Barcelona - shrapnel,' he shrugged.

Eva touched her old friend's cheek tenderly.

'Please let me buy you lunch, how are you?'

Dariusz Szpilman took a light from Eva and exhaled, his right hand tapping the ash lightly. Since losing his left arm, she noted, his right cheek had developed a tic. Some of the ash missed the ashtray and blew away on the draught from the café's door. He brushed some of it off his coat, his first impulse being to use his left hand. The inability to do this simple act depressed him further.

The lunchtime rush hour had abated and they were alone, apart from a bored looking waitress staring out through the window. His shoulders were a little rounded for a young man and he was more slumped in the chair.

To him, Eva looked even more beautiful than he remembered her being, even at the beach near Nice where he had seen her golden body in a bathing suit. In the trenches of Catalonia at times it was her shimmering image that kept him going. It sustained him through the rain, blistering heat and make-shift hospital where he was rushed after the explosion. The Russian surgeon, exhausted by his day's workload, had more hacked off his arm than cut it. Dariusz had been conscious throughout, pinned down by the shoulders and legs, brandy poured down his throat to numb him. He hallucinated for days after the amputation, imagining Eva coming to him as an angel to mop his fevered brow. Flying above him with the elegant wings of a swan, she seemed to lift him by the hand, holding his head close to her breasts.

As he was convalescing from his injuries, he was approached to join the Polish secret service. His cameras had been shipped back to Warsaw and some of the images became intelligence documents. Once fully recovered and back in Warsaw, Dariusz set out to assemble a team of operatives. Eva was an ideal choice because of her language skills. He had located her through the Krakow University attendance registers.

Travelling to the university, he had spotted her. His heart began to race as she strode across the campus. There was a maturity about her, and knowing her habits from their days in Paris, he rightly guessed which bookstore in Warsaw she would visit.

He had followed her from a distance, boarding the same train as she had, staying a carriage back, occasionally walking through, ensuring she didn't get off at any stop. He watched her as she made her way through the station, her hips swaying beneath her recognisable blue raincoat. She was sourcing some titles for the library and he caught his breath at the sound of her voice again as she spoke to the sales clerk.

Pretending to browse for a title, with a weight in his throat, he approached her and eventually gathered his courage to speak to her. He was deflated that she didn't recognise him straightaway, her eyes trying to recall his face, a smile indifferently fixed in place.

Seated in the café, he asked after Theo, but Eva shrugged nonchalantly. After the initial small talk, Dariusz lowered his voice and got to the point. 'Eva, how would you feel about working for our government? We need someone to go to London on our behalf, someone with fluent English.' He reached into his coat and placed an envelope onto the table. Eva opened it. Inside was a new Dutch passport requiring a photograph, a Dutch press pass, Dutch travel documents and airline tickets.

'Our friends the British have helped us with the journalist card.'

Eva was taken aback at his sudden change from friend to something quite remote and distant. Something was cold behind his eyes. It was a pain she could recognise. It was warping him and she idly wondered if his eyes were a mirror to her own soul. She could almost see the same darkness touching the corneas of his eyes.

He glanced around the café. The bored waitress had gone back into the kitchen leaving them alone. He stared into her eyes: They were grey yet capable of projecting warmth, her auburn hair long again and fashioned into a ponytail. Her mouth mesmerised him: He had heard her voice almost every night in his dreams. He wanted to blurt out that he loved her, had loved her since the day they met in the university bar, introduced by the louche artiste Theo. But the moment passed and he tried to focus.

From the depths of his side coat pocket he produced a photograph. He paused. He felt an awful pang of regret for his next words even before they were uttered.

It had taken time, a lot of digging into the bureaucratic static that existed between Poland and Germany. It wasn't lost on him that he was probably the only one-armed Polish spy in Europe, but he had to see Eva just one more time in the flesh, to hear her voice and catch the faintest whiff of her perfume. Then he would disappear, slip into the shadows and become a section chief, sending the likes of Eva to certain death.

'You might remember this man here,' he said, pushing the photograph toward her, 'Jurgen Locher.'

She shrugged, no.

'Arrested in Berlin in 1933, was released after six months in prison for assaulting a Herr Jan Gruber, a highly regarded German theatre director and the possible assault of an unknown Polish student at a Berlin University. Locher's father is a high-ranking member of the Nazi party and got him out with a pardon if he served in Spain with the Fascists.'

Eva sucked her breath involuntarily and looked away, blinking sudden scalding tears. Daruisz reached out and touched her hand tenderly. She snapped it away. She remembered the leer of her assailants' faces. She had played over and over in her head various scenarios about what would have happened had she remained with Jonas that night that made her shudder. She wanted revenge. She wanted Locher stone cold dead.

She took the photograph, dabbing tears from her eyes. It was him, the one with the small eyes. Instinctively she touched the part of her head where he had ripped the hair out.

'Locher is now an Obersturmbannführer serving as a special advisor to Franco in Spain. He has been entrusted with a delivery of gold bullion from Spain's gold reserves to Berlin to pay for German weapons and armaments. We must alert the British that it may affect their position in the Mediterranean.'

'Why not a diplomat?' she asked, beginning to regain her composure,

'We lost a courier a few days ago. We need someone who isn't on a Gestapo list.' He studied her expression before leaning in and stating in earnest. 'We can't have another Fascist dictator strutting around Europe spreading their poison from the Atlantic to the Baltic Eva.'

'What about another Stalin, Dariusz?' she countered.

Dariusz gave a smile. It was as cold as a morgue. 'If you are successful on this occasion, we may have more work for you.'

Eva thought for a moment. Her lust for revenge was setting her on a course that would alter her life entirely. Maybe she had no choice now as Europe was being set alight and everyone was being gradually sucked into the flames. Seeing Dariusz again brought back many happy memories despite the embittered ending with Theo.

She could see a fervour coming back into Dariusz's deadened eyes when he mentioned Spain. Maybe she could make a difference somehow; maybe her actions would end Locher and his ilk, maybe stop another girl mourning a dead lover before it was too late.

She didn't trust Dariusz, but made her mind up anyway. 'Ok, I'll do it. But I want Locher's address in Spain.'

'The man you are to contact is a Henry Chainbridge. The document in question was delivered to your room in the university, folded into today's London Times.' As an afterthought he added, 'By the way, Eva, can you use a gun?'

The newspaper, as Dariusz had said, was under her door. She felt a faint sense of violation that Dariusz knew where she was living. Leafing through it, she came across the crossword. The solution had been filled in with numbers and symbols in pen. Beneath the solution was an address in London in the same hand-writing that had filled out the crossword. The bullion shipment would be happening within a month which gave her adequate time to prepare, Dariusz had said as he handed her the money to pay for the trip in the various denominations.

After dinner Eva rooted out maps and atlases from her bookshelves, a habit she had picked up from her father. Every one of her weekend cycling trips was carefully plotted out and she got a sense of sheer enjoyment of completing a journey that she had meticulously planned.

The following day, she went to the university library and took out more maps and travel guides, and through the university switchboard made enquiries with the German National bus service. Also through the university she sent a telegram to Madame Yvette, signing it off as 'Hannah Du Trop', a character Dariusz had devised for one of his

8mm shorts in Paris. It would stick in Yvette's mind as they had performed their lines strapped to high-backed chairs. Eva assumed he'd be tracking her movements and this is a character he too would remember. There was enough money supplied by Dariusz, but as a precaution she withdrew double the amount in case of unforeseen problems.

She spent the evening poring over the books and maps and with both Polish and German bus timetables, devising a circuitous route that would take three days to complete, ending in Paris. She assumed the Gestapo would be watching every railway station and airport; on a bus she could blend into a group or get off at the first sign of danger .With this in mind, she picked the earliest and latest departure times. The nagging thought was that she could either be bait or a diversion for another courier with the real intelligence, however deciding that she was going to do this and do it well, she resigned herself to the task. She took her knapsack down from her wardrobe, rolled her blue raincoat up and fixed it to the straps. Then she folded and packed the maps with the relevant time tables written out on their margins. From her touring days in the theatre she packed clothing for three days' travel – every item black.

After a good breakfast, she put on a heavy jumper and an old coat she was planning to jettison, eschewing her make-up bag. Madame Yvette would have ample amounts of that for her to use when she got there. Finally for the journey, she selected a novel and a flannel cloth for her face so as to be able to freshen up in the station toilets.

She set out on her bicycle for the main bus station and, as she pedalled, felt a sudden surge of excitement. It felt a bit like acting, dressing up for the part. She smoked a quick cigarette before her departure, sensing that it would be a long time before she saw this city again.

Three days later she was at the establishment of Madame Yvette, who welcomed her with a radiant smile. 'Well...?'

Eva sat on the edge of the immense bath in her private quarters. She marvelled at how delicious a bath was after a long journey. Again she dipped below the surface, relishing its heat. Yvette had disposed of the old coat, had a new wardrobe waiting for her and fresh make-up, and had set up a spare bed in her room away from the working girls where Eva would spend the night.

'I had one problem on the border with a policeman, though once he saw my journalist card and note books, he believed I was a travel writer.'

'They'll believe anything from a pretty mouth,' exhaled Yvette, her cigarette smoke seeming to linger around her, her lush tresses falling down around her face, framing her classic profile. Eva hadn't noticed before what a beautiful woman she was without make-up.

Yvette procured at Eva's request maps and timetables for the train to the Calais ferry and over dinner they reviewed the best options. Yvette handed Eva a sheet with a crudely drawn map of England with place names underlined and relevant ferry, bus and rail departure times jotted in. Eva had joked about using a gun and Yvette, with a twinkle in her eye, went out of the bathroom and returned with her prized stiletto. 'Please take this. I have another one here. Remember, Eva, always aim at the heart or the balls.'

From the Gare du Nord she took the early morning train and overnight ferry to the south of England, again using early morning and late evening timetables.

She found the London address up a discreet mews off Oxford Street by early afternoon. As she entered through the door, a small bell jingled and a tall thin man in his fifties looked up from the shop counter. It was a book shop with lines of shelves stacked to the brim. She fell in love with place immediately.

'Can I help you, miss?'

'Yes, I wonder if you can help me, please. I'm looking for a book entitled 'Samizdat'.'

'I'm afraid we don't have that publication, but I can recommend 'War and Peace'.' It was the correct response.

Eva handed him her paperback; inside it was the crossword cut out from the newspaper.

'We've been expecting you, Miss Molenaar,' and after a pause while the man studied what she had handed him, 'Oh this is excellent. This information is invaluable, priceless.'

Henry Chainbridge introducing himself formally and immediately invited Eva to spend the night in private lodgings above the shop so that she could rest before returning to Poland, throwing in the incentive of freshly laundered bedding and warm water to bathe in. He regretted that he himself would be returning home for the night and would therefore be reprehensibly deficient as a host, but he hoped that she would be comfortable nonetheless. She assured him that she was used to coping on her own. He then made a series of phone calls. He had arranged a plate of sandwiches and fresh tea for her which sat on the modest wooden dresser. Exhausted from the journey, Eva retired to bed and fell into a fitful sleep soon after Chainbridge's departure.

The next morning, Eva rose early and descended the steps to the shop. She looked around at the bees-waxed shelves and musty books which gave the room the same sense of being a sanctuary as her father's library had at home.

She found Mr. Chainbridge poring over the morning paper which was spread across the shop counter. He heard her footfall, looked up and smiled. 'Let's get some breakfast, Miss Molenaar.'

She was alone in this vast metropolis, yet felt she could trust him. He wore a wedding band and was as attentive to her as a kindly professor, giving off an erudite air of contentment as he closed up his shop. He led her to an early morning café situated amid the bustle of market stalls and taxi drivers. It buzzed with breakfast banter, the rattle of crockery, and shouts and blasts of steam from the kitchens,

Chainbridge explained the situation. 'The Spanish Prime Minister Negrin has sanctioned gold bullion shipments to the Soviet Union as payment for weapons and advisors. A portion of it has been intercepted by Franco. He's diverting it to either a German port or a country friendly with the Nazi regime.'

Chainbridge studied the young woman. Eva held his gaze intently. A sixth sense in him detected a secondary agenda within the girl.

'We think the ship involved is British registered, but can't be sure. We need to understand what is happening down there, study their operations as a precaution against future eventualities. You could be of great assistance if you would be willing to be so. Would you be interested in remaining here for a day or two and attending a private party?'

Eva thought about this abrupt change of plan, this level of additional involvement for which she had not remotely been prepared. She had confirmed to Spzilman that she had arrived safely and was awaiting further instructions. So far she'd received no response. It would be interesting to see more of this country and whatever she was required to do could hardly be that dangerous. Nevertheless, she wondered.

'Certainly, if I can be of any help.' Her English was almost flawless. Chainbridge smiled warmly. She could be just what he needed. They were getting closer to mapping several of the Nazi spy rings in London. There was no threat of war as such, yet there was a faction in the British security community who believed that Hitler was considerably more dangerous long term than he was currently being considered to be by their political masters. Franco was a more impressive character than Hitler but far less dangerous because Spain was a relatively small country currently ravaged by civil war. If Hitler started to throw his weight around on the world stage, Franco would almost certainly be an ally given all the weaponry Germany was providing him with, and all suggestions to date were that the German agents and their Nationalist Spanish counterparts were a bit lackadaisical and therefore an excellent source of information on Berlin's strategic and tactical thinking if they could infiltrate them.

Chainbridge hesitated and his nose quivered pinkly. He coughed embarrassedly and gave indications of being reluctant to start his next sentence. 'This is a bit indelicate,' he stammered hesitantly, 'but vital for our cause .... ' He paused an awkwardly long time for effect while he searched Eva's face in an unexpectedly shrewd manner. This was no antiquarian biblbiophile. Chainbridge was something else but well disguised. 'I've had the presumption to book you provisionally into a small hotel off Grosvenor Square where a certain Lord Alfred Bevansdale likes to trawl for girls.'

Eva stared at him. 'For girls?' She raised an eyebrow.

'You might be his type, for a party he's throwing.'

'His type?' Eva raised a second eyebrow and lit up a cigarette as she spoke, stirring her tea slowly. Even without make-up, and with her hair in a pony tail, she still attracted glances. 'What type would that be?'

'Show girls, chorus line, starlet types. Lord Alfred Bevansdale is a cigarette baron and a Fascist sympathiser, a close friend of Sir Oswald Mosley's, and we suspect that he has offered the Nationalists a ship to transfer the bullion mixed in with one of his own consignments. Naturally, we can do nothing about this, even should we wish to, but it is nonetheless an opportunity for us. However, if you are not comfortable with this, Miss Molenaar ....'

She exhaled slowly from the side of her mouth, her expression hardening. 'How old is he?'

'Early fifties, there or thereabouts,'

'I can't see any problem, Mr Chainbridge.'

Chainbridge visibly relaxed. 'So long as you are sure,' he added, pressing his luck to ensure that Eva was truly on board.

'I am sure.'

'Very good. Let's finish up here. Waiter!' He scribbled discreetly into the air to indicate he wished to pay the bill. The waiter acknowledged his request with a nod.

Eva was daunted by her task. She had been briefed as to what Chainbridge wanted, to know where the bullion would be loaded, who the main operators would be, who was over-seeing the planning of the transfer from Berlin.

Why would Lord Bevansdale be interested in her? It was an outside chance that he would even notice her, however pretty she was. Did she really look like a show girl?

In the event, ensnaring Lord Bevansdale proved much easier than Eva had expected. The following night she had positioned herself conspicuously at the end of the hotel bar where he could clearly see her should he turn up. Unbeknown to her, from a small room where he was playing poker, Bevansdale spied her immediately in her vivid emerald dress that clung to her figure. Within minutes he was over to her, all smiles and champagne.

With a sigh of relief, Eva expertly charmed him in return. Within the hour, Lord Bevansdale had invited her to his party, which was to be a masked ball to be held at his mansion deep in the heart of the English countryside and, to ensure her attendance, he had offered to escort her there in person and offered to buy her outfit for the event and for the rest of the weekend besides.

Eva was slightly surprised that Lord Bevansdale would not be at the party from the beginning to greet his guests but he explained that the whole thing would be a dreadful bore and if she wasn't there it would hardly be worth attending at all.

* * *

Bevansdale's mansion blazed gloriously through the windshield of his chauffer-driven Rolls Royce as they swept down the driveway which was festooned with ribbons and lights draped along the trees and edges.

'Here we are, my dear,' he boomed.

He was short, portly, florid from gout and mashed into a dinner suit. Eva was dressed in fur, a new low-cut black dress and a diamond encrusted cat mask. Bevansdale's hand had a tremor every time it brushed her. He was also sweating.

Liveried footmen bowed as they alighted from the car and entered the doorway. The chauffeur would see their luggage to their respective rooms. A vast stairway ascended toward a hallway bedecked in a massive crystal chandelier. In rooms off the main reception, the guests mingled in all varieties of expensive dress, the men middle-aged, their companions mostly young women. In the main dining room a string quartet was performing Vivaldi, resplendent in period costume up to their powdered wigs and, like the rest of the guests, all masked. Excusing herself, Eva enquired where the toilets were. A passing footman burdened with a tray laden with champagne nodded roughly in the direction of upstairs. Eva decided to get her bearings and took her time looking through the upper floors. In some of the bedrooms couples in various stages of undress were lolling on huge beds; others were engaged in more vigorous activities. She glanced past the heaving flesh around her, not quite sure what she was looking for but convinced she would know when she found it.

Entering the dining room she found Bevansdale in a corner with a group of men masked in black velvet almost like a uniform. One had a German accent and they all looked intimidating. They exuded power. Eva sidled up to Bevansdale, pressing against his arm. He flushed and almost gagged on his cigar. The others all turned to her, admiring her figure and the warm mouth smiling beneath her mask.

She whispered in his ear. 'You haven't shown me the bedrooms yet, Alfie?' She blew softly into his ear as he leered back. 'Forgive me for being so remiss. Allow me to escort you.'

She made a point of looking back at the group and smiling seductively beneath her mask before turning her back and guiding Bevansdale upstairs. As they left the room, she could feel the group's eyes following her. Bevansdale guided her to a narrow staircase which led past the upper floors to his private quarters. His private study was dark panelled and spartanly furnished. He led her to an oaken door at the far side of the room. With a wink he produced a key from the watch chain on his waist coat and opened the door. It was a small bedroom near the top floor, smelling faintly of mothballs and dust. A four-poster bed hewn in dark mahogany stood in the middle of the room,

'Oh Alfie, this is perfect,' Eva breathed. 'I can't think of anything nicer.'

* * *

Before returning to the shop to meet Mr. Chainbridge, Eva took the cat mask to a jeweller's. The diamonds encrusting the mask were indeed real, as Lord Beavansdale had promised. Poor Alfie. She exchanged half of them for cash; the other half she kept on her for emergencies, hidden in a locket around her neck.

'The ship is the Adelaide, a merchant ship outward bound from Southampton and arriving in Marseilles in three weeks' time. The bullion is arriving from Cadiz. It will be loaded in Marseilles and delivered in Hamburg. I have written down the details.'

Chainbridge whistled quietly.

'May I ask how you got the information?' he enquired.

Eva smiled at him coyly. 'A lady must have her secrets. However, I can guarantee that nobody realises that I have learnt anything.'

Chainbridge took the piece of paper she passed to him, scanned it quickly and whistled again. 'Excellent, Eva, thank you. Now, I have another task for you, should you agree to accept it.'

'What would you have me do now?' she asked somewhat sharply.

'We would like you to go to Spain?'

'Spain?' Now Eva was interested.

'Of course, if you do not feel up for it ....'

'I'm listening. I assume you want me to learn more about the German and Nationalist network down there.'

'Not just a pretty face,' Mr. Chanbridge commented appreciatively. 'Exactly. You are not a known operative. You are not even British. Nobody there will realise that your government is in any way involved in this.'

'So what do I do?'

'A colleague of ours, Mr. De Witte, will be here shortly. He will accompany you to Southampton and brief you. From Southampton you will return to Paris and make contact with a a Soviet advisor named 'Spassky' who will escort you to Spain and brief you further from their perspective along the way. The objective is to learn as much about their operations as possible, who are their liaisons in Berlin and how they communicate with them. And I wish you the very best of luck. You are a very plucky girl. I wish you were one of ours.'

Twenty minutes later Eva was collected in a taxi by De Witte who, to her surprise, was blind and, even more to her surprise, proved to be excellent company. The ferry from Sothampton took her to Calais and from there she travelled on to Paris where Yvette supplied her with a gun and Eva arranged to meet 'Spassky' who turned out to be a female Russian agent based in Barcelona. They were to travel together. At the Gare D'Austerlitz they both took the Perpignan train, and from there crossed the Pyrenees into Spain posing as journalists.

Chapter 4

London, 1938

Henry Chainbridge sat back deep into the leather chair. The rain was lashing the windows of his small chambers above his shop, Chainbridge Books, *'Fine prints and antiquities a speciality'*. Opposite him on a well-worn leather sofa sat Eva and her handler, Peter De Witte. Both looked drained from the train journey out of Germany, across France and over the Channel.

Eva was one of three agents he had sent to Munich and the only one to return alive. A silver pot of coffee and fine china were placed on a low table by an Indian woman dressed in a brightly coloured sari. As quietly as she appeared, she slipped back into the shadows with a discreet bow.

Eva's information ahead of their arrival had raised eyebrows in Whitehall: Poland was to be divided between Germany and Russia. The Soviets had commenced a new rail link using gulag labour beneath the city of Moscow itself. They were also involved in deep mining near the city of Tyumen, in Siberia, again for unspecified reasons. Despite the rapprochement between the Soviet Union and Germany, Stalin did not trust Hilter an inch.

Chainbridge let his cigarette burn down to the filter before stubbing it out. In the event of an attack, Lenin's tomb would be a priority evacuation, probably to Tyumen. He re-read the last sentence, slowly blowing out smoke.

'Are they serious..?' His voice was warm, whiskey and tobacco mellowed, and hinted a university education. There were still traces of his native Belfast accent when he spoke at length.

Eva noted that behind him, on his long bookshelves in pristine lines, stood leather-bound ancient Greek and Cyrillic embossed books like her grandfather's. A print of Johan Sebastian Bach hung on the far wall in a broad gilded mount frame. Beneath it, objets d'art from India stood alongside notebooks, paintbrushes and pencils. A phonograph sat against the far wall, with Shellac discs glistening in their sleeves. Fragile music manuscripts lay under glass and discreetly illuminated on tables beside an upright piano. From time-to-time Eva had sat at the piano recalling preludes learnt as a child, helping her unwind from assignments. This room always made her feel safe, reminding her of her grandfather's study. It had that same smoky, tumble-down feel.

'Apparently they value a corpse over a civilian population,' said Eva, crossing her long legs.

It's a pity Peter can't see the beauty beside him, thought Chainbridge. In the lamplight, her auburn hair glowed like a halo, her cheekbones shadowing down to a warm generous mouth. She reminded Chainbridge of a Da Vinci study.

Peter sat still, head inclined, in an immaculate slate-grey suit, fine-tuned to the nuances in the room. A deep scar ran across his face, temple to temple, which in the shadows gave the appearance of folding in on itself. It almost added to his good looks.

'I suppose Lenin's a beacon to half the world's proletariat, a psychological blow to the Soviets if anything should happen to him,' said Chainbridge, skimming the salient points.

'A propaganda coup,' agreed Peter. His timbre was deep, the tone clipped. Chainbridge leaned forward looking into Eva's wide-set grey eyes.

'How drunk was this attaché?'

'Very ... but in a Russian's case, drunkenness is relative. He didn't slur a word. They believe that an attack is inevitable, it is only a question of when, and they are preparing for it,'

Chainbridge closed her report pensively. Her hunch seemed to square with what another agent had uncovered - schematics for a new type of Zeppelin being commissioned by Goering in readiness for an attack of the Soviet Union. If Chainbridge had this information, then he assumed his NKVD counterpart would have it too. Hitler was signing non-aggression pacts with Stalin and Von Ribbentrop was strutting around Europe with reams of treaty drafts under his arm. Confetti and smokescreens.

He removed his glasses deliberately as if a solution would present itself before he put them back in their case.

Anti-Soviet agents were assisting the Nazi war machine and every spy agency in Europe was using Berlin as its hub. Berlin, in turn, was trying to neutralise what they considered to be enemy agents almost as soon as they set foot on German soil. What they had here could be misinformation - it could be something or it could be nothing. Hitler, like Comrade Joe, was skilled at keeping everyone guessing. Snatching Lenin from under the Soviet's nose was one thing; Hitler had a flair for the dramatic. Invading Poland, though, that would precipitate an international crisis.

'Number 10 won't buy it. I know Chamberlain. He believes Hitler has gone as far as he needs to go. He thinks Versailles has been put to bed.' Chainbridge rose to his feet, his long frame and receding grey hairline gave him a slightly avian appearance. 'Besides, Chamberlain thinks we've achieved peace in our time,'

Both men smiled ruefully at that remark. Eighteen years earlier, Henry Chainbridge and Peter De Witte had fought against the Red Army during the Russian Civil War, an Englishman and a Dutchman fighting side-by-side with other nations until De Witte was blinded by grenade shrapnel at Arkhangelsk as the allied forces were routed by the Bolsheviks.

They hadn't exchanged a single word until that moment when Peter fell screaming in pain, clutching what was left of his face after the grenade exploded. However, afterwards, Henry had stayed with him, practically dragging him through the frozen tundra to the port of Murmansk for evacuation to England. For three weeks De Witte had endured the agony with only sips of vodka and the odd lukewarm watery coffee to act as painkillers. Salt biscuits and stale bread dipped in tea were forced into his mouth, For most of the journey he had wanted to die. Henry had sat with him through this voyage, holding his hand and talking. He had kept him alive. When it suited him, Chainbridge could talk, spinning yarns from dusk till dawn. He'd been an endless stream of tales from his native Belfast, switching to memorised quotations from Chaucer, Shakespeare and W.B Yeats. Bringing him home to Oxford, he had stayed with De Witte through his gradual recuperation.

A linguistics professor before enlisting, De Witte found a part-time position in the classics faculty at the university. There he met and eventually married a fellow Dutch academic, Martha Vermeer. She became his nurse, his lover and his eyes, a steady North Star through his pain and anger. She helped him learn Braille and they moved to Utrecht in the late 1920s where they took lecturing roles at the university there. Their marriage allowed him to rediscover his vocation as a teacher, a vocation he had abandoned once he took up arms and joined the Allied Expeditionary force in response to the Russian Revolution.

But he was restless, longing for the thrill of adventure and exploration, challenging in his own words 'the limits of his limits'. The couple drifted apart and by the early 1930s De Witte found himself back lecturing in Oxford alone. Martha steadfastly refused to divorce him.

By that time, Chainbridge had been approached by MI5 and B5B to create a cell monitoring Communist sympathisers in the nation's universities. He asked De Witte to join him. The Dutchman's aural senses had become acute as compensation for his loss of sight, and he could sit stock still for hours, focusing on conversations picked up on hidden microphones. He was fascinated by linguistics and being a natural polyglot began developing a cipher code based on Braille. Throughout the 1930s the two men built a small operating unit of spies who were discreet and highly effective.

Then De Witte asked MI6 about the possibility of going to Spain just as the country convulsed into civil war. His request was refused and he remained in London, assisting MI6 to monitor communications and code-breaking messages sent by both sides in the civil war, especially the Soviet Union's codes.

He had escorted Eva to Southampton at the start of her first mission and from that journey their relationship had flourished despite their rarely having occasion to meet each other in person. The result of the operation had been that Chainbridge had gained invaluable insights into German, Soviet and Spanish undercover operations.

Chainbridge also knew that later that year, in Barcelona, Eva had killed Locher, one of the key German operatives she was monitoring, after he had confronted her with his discovery that she was spying for Polish and British intelligence, or so she had said. However, Chainbridge's ever-sharp intuition told him that Eva was working another agenda, perhaps on the instructions of her Polish masters. Whatever the true facts, Chainbridge was duly encouraged that this beautiful lady could be as cold-blooded and lethal as any successful operative would have to be to survive in the field. She was also an accomplished translator, fluent in Russian, Polish, German, Dutch and English.

Chainbridge had been unable to uncover much about her life before she visited him in London that first time other than that her grandfather was a celebrated Dutch intellectual. However, since her return from Spain to Poland, she had appeared in a film produced by an avant-garde director in Warsaw, had toured Europe in an experimental theatre group, and then disappeared for a year, reappearing after being screen tested personally by Goebbels who had spotted her at a cabaret in Berlin. Presumably in line with her Polish secret service guidance, she had begun to cultivate an image of an occasional, but gifted, actress on the look-out for a rich man. This allowed her to move in the privileged circles of the Nazi party élite. Her beauty and confidence meant there was always a man in attendance. Her smile, the kind that starts in the eyes, had an effect on men that was undlilutedly chemical. They would literally do anything she wanted. Perhaps that was why she was drawn to Peter; he couldn't see her.

Did De Witte ever get jealous about Eva's professional affairs? No, Chainbridge thought not. He and De Witte were too wise to let petty emotions get in the way, well aware of the morass Europe was sliding into.

Chainbridge turned away from them allowing them a private moment together. Staring out at the autumnal rain streaming down the window panes, he asked, 'Tell me more about this Donald T Kincaid chap, Eva.'

* * *

Guy Maynard Liddle of B5B section looked up from his desk at Chainbridge after reading the assessment from Eva and De Witte. As

Chainbridge's immediate superior; he answered to Department head Vernon Kell, who in turn answered to the Foreign Office and effectively the Prime Minister.

The summer rain had been pouring out of the heavens in titanic bursts, washing Whitehall in a deluge, flooding its corridors and rooms with an unseasonal gloom. Chainbridge had risen early and driven through the rush hour traffic. London, bustling as ever, was glistening in the early morning light. Eva and De Witte had left his chambers for a safe house near Kensington to unwind. Later that week they would be guests of Oswald and Diana Mosley at a BUF rally, maintaining their cover as journalists sympathetic to the Fascist cause.

He ascended the steps to a discreet doorway on King Charles Street and was ushered through the Georgian foyer, past the armed serviceman who saluted him, to Liddle's office. It was a small room off a non-descript corridor, filled with the smell of beeswax and tobacco, and peppered with maps of Europe around the walls. In common with Chainbridge's chambers, it was piled high with sensitive intelligence from all over Europe. Unlike Chainbridge's chambers, it had no windows. Chainbridge couldn't function without being able to observe the seasons and marvelled at Liddle's fortitude. He never left this broom closet.

The room, like the corridor, was as quiet as a monastic cell. The whole environment here made Chainbridge feel uneasy, the slow pace and old school tie feel of the place. From these corridors, ministers directed soldiers and spies, sometimes deliberately, to their deaths for the greater good of the Empire. He was an old soldier who found the peacetime uncomfortable, yet he never wished to see wholesale slaughter again.

He stood beside the desk, refusing the chair he was offered. He always preferred to stand before a superior.

'Henry, how solid is this?'

Chainbridge assumed his intelligence was being dismissed out of hand. He bristled. 'Miss Molinaar has a better insight into the way a Russian mind works than we have. This Russian attaché is well connected within the Politburo at a political and family level. I trust her judgement. And we still have no word as to the whereabouts of Leonard and McGowan. We're assuming the Gestapo intercepted them.'

Liddle hummed tunelessly for a moment as he reviewed the dossier. There was a possible redoubt beyond the Urals and no-one to verify it. He trusted Chainbridge's views; he wouldn't have come to him with this without due consideration.

Chainbridge and De Witte had broken several Communist rings operating within the Oxbridge universities. Now B5B section's focus was Oswald Mosley and his bunch of thugs. Mosley could yet be a British Hitler or Mussolini in the making should a war ever break out. The section was juggling the forces of the extreme right and the extreme left, both Leviathans heading on a collision course across Europe. B5B was underfunded and understaffed, and Liddle seemed to be the only one, apart from Chainbridge and Churchill, who could foresee that Germany might disregard any kind of peace treaty.

Added to his woes, the Admiralty was vying for the counter-espionage brief and the glamorous tars seemed to have the upper hand with the current government. Liddle sighed inwardly. The shinier the brocade on the epaulettes, the more likely counter-intelligence would be moving off his desk. He was a policeman at heart, which meant hard graft and footwork, and the pain-staking gathering of evidence.

'I'll pass it up the chain of command, but don't get your hopes up. Chamberlain believes he's got Hitler where he wants him.'

Chainbridge turned to leave, Liddle rose also. The rain seemed to be increasing in volume outside, the din almost drowning out his voice.

'Henry, as you know we're struggling to improve the network. With too few operatives in the field that we can trust, we will need Miss Molinaar back in mainland Europe. The Polish authorities have requested that she be returned to them and that suits our purposes too. De Witte will have to remain here. I need the two of you to start putting feelers out across the country for operatives. You and I know there's a war coming and that maniac in Berlin wants to set the world alight. We need to be prepared,'

Chainbridge nodded slowly. Liddle handed him a dossier,

'Supplied to us by the Yanks. Mister Donald T Kincaid will be in Berlin a week from today depositing some of his considerable fortune into Hitler's coffers. Miss Molinaar is to strike up a relationship with Kincaid as a joint mission between ourselves and the Poles, and remain with him as his companion. He has transferred an enormous amount of money lately and we don't have the why's, where's or how's. He's an open supporter of Hitler and stands on the first amendment in all of his outbursts when questioned about it.'

Chainbridge skimmed the first few paragraphs: D.T. Kincaid, film magnate, many media interests - newsreels, newspapers, periodicals and advertising. Some of the photographs were from London where he was searching for his next big star. Amid all the doom and gloom of the papers, a man of this magnitude was bringing the Technicolor razzmatazz of Hollywood to Britain. A very, very rich man; political too.

'I'll talk to Miss Molinaar.'

Liddle dialled the Foreign Office extension as Chainbridge left.

'Hello, yes, I'd like to talk to the Minister. We have a bit of an oddity here, might be worth following up on. Something our friends the Russians might be up to.'

Chapter 5

Oswald Mosley was in his element, surrounded by journalists, hangers on and well-wishers. Despite the waning fortunes of the British Union of Fascists, he still managed to be newsworthy and pull a crowd. It was more of a banquet than a rally, with long benches and tables stretching the length of the converted cellar down along the London's docklands. It reminded Eva of a German beer hall.

A podium stood on a stage at one end, flanked by the red, white and blue flags of his party. Granite-faced Blackshirts formed a line in front of the stage, with matching black batons resting between their hands, a necessity after the last rally was broken up by rampaging Jews, Communists and Irish Dockers in protest at his extreme right wing manifesto.

Eva and De Witte were introduced to him by Diana Mosley and Eva noted that he and Peter had similarities. Mosley was dashing, rake thin and with a mischievous twinkle in his eye. He appraised Eva in a single glance, slowly exhaling his cigarette smoke as he did so.

'Hello again,' he smiled. 'Munich a few weeks ago? I never forget a pretty face.'

She held his gaze to Diana's discomfort and allowed him to kiss her hand which he did as smoothly as a libertine. In his black uniform, webbing and jodhpurs, he resembled a lounging fighter pilot or suave Hollywood leading man. Eva produced her camera, a

German Leica, and took a few shots. He posed gallantly, his eyes never leaving her.

De Witte cleared his throat and pushed his way through the press corps. He held a leather-bound board with blank paper clipped to it. A long stylus chained to it made grooves into the paper as he jotted in shorthand. Discreet wires running across the board allowed him to ensure straight lines as he wrote, using his thumb to tell him where to place the next line.

Mosley observed he, like most of the aristocrats attending, was sympathetic to King Edward's plight in Spain, that he might in fact be the rightful King of England.

De Witte retorted, 'So if war was declared, a more sympathetic monarch to the Fascist crusade may be more acceptable to the British population?' He then followed on, 'How do you plan to depose the current monarch? A French or Russian style revolution perhaps?'

Ignoring De Witte, Mosley introduced his Italian and German SS guests beside him who saluted straight armed in the flash of bulbs. He told the press he believed that the United Kingdom, Germany and Italy were potential allies against the rise of Communism. His Fascist brothers from Europe were here tonight attending the dinner in solidarity with the BUF and the people of the United Kingdom. They shared his belief that Germany and England would not go to war against each other again, citing the willingness of Westminster to appease Hitler.

Then in a sudden flare of anger Mosley launched into a diatribe against the Soviet Union, the Communists and repeated the 'fact' that he, Hitler and Mussolini were bulwarks in Europe against this menace.

Bounding athletically onto the stage as he spoke and striding to the podium, he gripped it in white-knuckled rage. The microphone carried his voice, giving it a tinny quality. Eva removed the flash from her camera and, clipping on the customised B5b wide angle lens, took discreet photographs of those attending. The room offered sufficient light she judged as she captured the German and Italian delegates speaking to the assembled guests. Lords, ladies, businessmen, some from the munitions industries, and bankers were captured on film. Some openly posed for her, believing their faces would be in periodicals across Europe the following week.

De Witte enquired as to how the BUF was being funded, the rumour being Mussolini was their big backer. Mosley laughed this off as 'Communist propaganda', saying it was the British working man in the street funding them, with generous private donations.

Some of the journalists scoffed out loud and Mosley's smile, though broad, slipped smoothly to a sneer. Eva noted that's where the similarities with De Witte ended. De Witte again raised a question as to the whereabouts of William Joyce, whether or not he was still a party member returned to America or now living in Nazi Germany? Mosley stared evenly at De Witte who inclined his head to improve his hearing. Joyce hadn't left the BUF but was actively liaising with the German High Command on behalf of the party, replied Mosley.

There was a growing sense of suspicion creeping into his voice in his replies toward De Witte.

De Witte continued, 'As in the case of Ernst Rohm, right hand men have a habit of coming to a sticky end in Fascist movements. Is Joyce possibly floating in the Thames somewhere?'

Some of the press laughed again. Mosley insisted that Joyce was alive and well and working with Dr. Josef Goebbels. As he spoke, several Blackshirts moved in toward De Witte, summoned with a nod from Mosley. Eva tapped De Witte's knee with a warning code and he flashed a smile to Mosley that was both immediately disarming and charming. Naturally it'll be off the record, he assured him. Mosley grunted into his pewter tankard and waved the men away. They dumbly obliged.

Diana and Unity Mitford stood beside her in breathless admiration of Oswald, his coconut oiled fringe flying free with every head shake. He held his audience in thrall and, at the end, all the guests raised their right arms in straight-armed salutes. Taking a deep breath he expanded his arms out in welcome and the assembly sat down to the meal. Diana was in raptures at the table and whispered into Eva's ear like a breathless schoolgirl, 'Please, please, Eva, come with us. Berlin is so beautiful, Adolf has done such wonders to the city. He has shown Oswald and me his plans for the New Berlin he plans to build. Really, really quite breath-taking,'

She studied Eva, a truly beautiful young woman and clearly in thrall to her older, handsome, blind companion. Eva had approached her weeks earlier asking to photograph her for a Dutch periodical. She had driven to Wooten Lodge through the rolling, beautiful countryside of Staffordshire and Diana had met her at the doorway personally. Eva glanced around at the tasteful furnishings and followed Diana into the drawing room.

Eva got the impression this frail girl spent a lot of time alone. Diana had warmed to her instantly, making her feel comfortable and remarked that she was surprised such a beautiful woman hadn't tried for the movies. With a blush, Eva had confided she had been studying for theatre and had toured Europe and was trying to break into the German film industry.

She had sent her portrait photo and resumé to Dr Joseph Goebbels in Berlin, reading that he was planning to establish a European film industry to match Hollywood. He had screen-tested her a few years earlier and her resumé was 'on file'.

The magazine shoot had gone well and in the process Eva and Diana had developed a friendship.

'Leave it to me, dear. I'll get Unity to talk to Adolf. They're very close,' She leaned in toward her, patting her knee. 'You belong on the silver screen, Miss Molenaar.'

Eva noted that Diana clipped the vowels in her name short. It sounded like 'Milner.' Eva decided she would use that as a pseudonym at some later stage.

Diana became a dedicated pen pal, sending letters to Eva regularly, the address a PO Box set up by M15 and B5b section. Once her letters were reviewed by Chainbridge, Eva would reply and would, where possible, slip in a direct query as to Oswald's whereabouts and plans. Diana knew she was being monitored, so little or no new information ever featured in her replies.

Eva felt guilty using Diana like this. She was drawn to the eccentric girl and found her fun to be around. Being an only child, Eva sometimes found it hard to build friendships, especially with women. Those who weren't intimidated by her beauty could be counted on one hand.

She watched the Mitfords with a hint of envy. She would have loved to have had a sister, be part of a big family. In time she vowed she would have one of her own as she watched the Mitfords laughing at a private joke.

Eva realised at that point she was lonely. Suddenly she wanted to flee home, a growing feeling she couldn't shake.

The banquet finished with Mosley and his men standing to attention, straight arm saluting and singing 'God Save the King' at the top of their lungs.

To Eva and De Witte it meant nothing; they had seen this scene across Europe. Diana was singing the loudest with tears in her eyes. Her sister Unity ran up to her and they hugged and cried together. Wiping away the tears, they turned to Eva and pleaded with her to fly to Berlin.

Amid the chants and shouts and belligerent songs Eva told them she would. The two girls posed for a photograph for Eva, two shimmering beauties amid the sea of black, red, white and blue.

Once she had the photographs she needed, Eva left, driving the car assigned to her and De Witte, handing the camera directly to Chainbridge's chambers for processing.

* * *

They flew into Berlin on a private charter funded by the BUF. Mosley sat a few rows ahead, flanked by his bodyguards, two beefy, shaven-headed Blackshirts. They stared straight ahead mutely while Mosley was reading the Financial Times, enjoying a brandy and a cigar. He was dressed in an immaculately cut black Saville Row herringbone double-breasted suit, French tailored shirt and patent leather shoes. In profile he resembled a hawk, with the same merciless eyes skimming the rise and fall of the money markets.

The three women had gone shopping for the visit two days earlier. Eva had enjoyed the whirl of dress shops, shoe shops and restaurants, and had to admit she got swept up in thrill of flying with such wonderful companions.

They were chauffeur driven through London and, as the streets glided past, Eva noted that sand bags had started appearing at the doorways and windows of certain government buildings.

Being in the company of the Mitford sisters, Eva got to see a world beyond her wildest dreams. First to Harrods, with fawning shop assistants and sections of the store closed off for their personal use. Then Oxford Street boutiques presenting them with haut coûture gowns, day wear and evening wear, and offers to alter their creations for Eva and the Mitfords.

Trays of champagne and canapés were given to them between showings, whether or not they wished to purchase anything. Every sales assistant told Eva her figure was perfect for modelling and the

Mitfords admitted they were jealous of her elegant build. Eva replied that she just wanted to be taken seriously as a photographer, and was envious of their gamine shape. Clothes seemed to hang much better on them.

Despite her protests, Diana wanted to buy Eva a shimmering silver evening dress as a gift, arguing the party they were going to was one of the biggest ever held in Germany.

Eva looked at her reflection in the dressing room. The gown was cut deep at the back, just stopping above her hips. The front wasn't cut as deep, but flattered the shape of her cleavage. The gloves had a matt silver look to them and Eva stopped Diana buying her accompanying jewellery, insisting she had complimentary accessories.

Eva had inherited a small fortune after her parents had been killed which she had transferred out of Poland to London on Chainbridge's advice. She insisted on paying for the dress and gloves. After a lot of persuasion, she accepted a clutch bag as a gift. Eva put her hair up and looked at her profile. The gown was exquisite, flattering her figure. She stepped out of the dressing room for the girls. They gasped and applauded with warm smiles and tilted champagne glasses.

'Why, dear, you could have your pick of the men if you wanted,' observed Unity, curious that Eva was enthralled with a much older blind man, albeit a handsome one, who was clearly much less enamoured of the Fascist cause than Eva was. In Unity's free hand dangled a pair of silver strap-up shoes with a modest heel. They complemented the dress perfectly.

Driving back through London where the chauffeur was going to bring her home, they asked Eva had she travelled much. She replied her work took her all around Europe, mostly freelance articles focusing on the rich and famous and their lifestyle. She then told them about her recent personal meeting with General Franco.

They offered to arrange an interview with Hitler for her magazine. He was very agreeable around pretty girls, Diana said, nudging Unity with a grin.

Diana spoke at length about the 'Strength through Joy' cruise she had taken last year with Eva Braun, Hitler's mistress. It was a pet project of Hitler, and Diana and Oswald had been privileged to have been invited on the maiden voyage along with high ranking members of the Nazi party

They had sailed around the Norwegian fjords, meeting their Aryan brothers and sisters. On board, the Propaganda Ministry had recorded the scenes in colour film to show across the cinemas of Germany, representing the Nordic countries as mountainous Aryan paradises.

The voyage had been a propaganda success and there was another voyage being planned. Eva was invited to join the sisters as their special guest and perhaps run a feature in one of the magazines she worked for.

Now they were descending through the clouds into the city that had driven her out five years ago, a city run by a maniac and his henchmen. The night before they had departed, she had dreamed of

Jonas, not uncommon, but this time more realistic.

She was in the morgue again, looking for him. She could hear him calling out to her from beneath the shrouds and she was pulling the sheets off to find him. Beneath every sheet removed was someone she knew; Papa, Mamma, Grampy and Aga, then Theo, Dariusz, De Witte - which disturbed her - and eventually she uncovered Jonas.

He was, as she remembered; dead, bloodied and broken, still on the gurney, but now dressed in a German Army uniform. Then suddenly his eyes opened wide, staring right at her, through her, his ruined mouth trying to talk.

She woke in a sweat, screaming.

The residue of the dream haunted her thoughts for the flight, putting her in a different world from the sisters who were chatting excitedly about the visit. Composing herself with a deep breath, she joined in and feigned joy at travelling around the most modern city in Europe.

Templehof Airport was busy as she descended the steps of the aircraft. Eva and the Mitfords watched the lines of international flights arriving and departing. Luftwaffe escort fighters taxied idly in lines, their pilots and crews lounging and standing in knots.

In the main terminal, she could hear British accents, French accents, and Swiss High German and Eastern European voices through the bustling arrivals area. Security was tight, with SS and Gestapo working alongside the police, everyone departing or arriving being subjected to questioning and identity checks. Once through the checks, they were greeted by a plain clothes party member who saluted them.

Mosley swept past him with barely a recognition; leaving it to Diana to make the introductions. His name was Otto Gottlieb and he had the careworn, nervous manner of an underling. Outside, a sleek plush Mercedes waited, with Nazi party flags flapping from the mudguards.

Mosley and the women sat in the back, the others following in a taxi behind. Eva's eyes glanced around the city. Humbolt University where Jonas had been thrown off a balcony swept past. It brought a sudden unexpected stab to her heart. Within minutes they were at the Chancellery.

They were ushered into Hitler's private chambers. He was regrettably unable to meet Herr Mosley, they were informed by his secretary, as he had an urgent matter to attend to. From beyond the door, there heard a man yelling, extolling and screaming out words, the door muffling what was being shouted.

'The Führer's practising for his speech tomorrow. He's spent hours rehearsing,' she explained with a cold but effective smile.

Mosley, momentarily wrong-footed, spun on his heel and barked over his shoulder as he strode from the room, 'I'll talk to him tonight!'

The door opened and a tall, grey-haired man of about sixty, dressed in Donegal tweed and knee-high brown boots, appeared. He looked flushed as if he had been doing all the shouting.

'You! Yeah you, miss. Get me tea, tea understand? – t-e-a with lots of honey. There's a honey!' He laughed at this.

The secretary turned, her face anxious.

78

'Quickly, doll! Adolf thinks he's losing his voice!'

She stepped back to her desk and phoned for tea to be delivered to the chambers. Eva held the man's gaze as he stared at her. 'Hello, Donald, we meet again. You don't remember me?' she made her smile very enticing and Donald T Kincaid returned the smile, ''fraid not, doll.' He clapped his hands louder. 'Schnell, schnell. Christ what's keeping you guys!'

Unity enquired gently, 'Is everything alright with Adolf?'

'Voice coaching. Giving him a little razzamatazz!'

'Gosh,' breathed Unity as Kincaid clapped his hands at the seething secretary. 'Schnell! Schnel, doll!'

As quickly as he appeared, he disappeared back into the room slamming the door.

Hitler's bodyguards glanced at one another then ushered the party out into the hall.

That night Eva struck up a longer conversation with Kincaid, enticing him away from their table to the bar. Hitler had cried off, complaining of laryngitis, sending his apologies for not attending, trying to save his voice. Eva Braun and her sister Gretl took the roles of hostess, a role they took to with relish.

Mosley's fury knew no bounds at being jilted a second time. His relationship with Hitler was strained at best. Hitler didn't speak English; Mosley didn't speak German. He sat at the table getting progressively more and more drunk and sullen. Diana, doing her best to lift his mood, was glancing mournfully at the churning dance floor.

Mosley's former right-hand man William Joyce joined them, a livid scar running from his lip to his ear, giving his smile an unnatural sneer, resplendent in full SS regalia. His American – Irish accent roared out to Kincaid who acknowledged him with a wave. Joyce was already drunk, sliding off his seat from time to time and rising up onto the table, clutching it like a drowning man, ordering another whiskey from any passing waiter.

The party was to celebrate the annexation of Austria, welcoming a lost people back into the fold, Hitler's kith and kin reunited with the German people. The room was festooned with Nazi flags and the flag of the Austrian Eagle. An orchestra was playing a number of up-beat polkas and waltzes beneath them.

The dance floor was thronged with swirling skirts and rigid uniforms, all moving to the beat of the music. Eva scanned the room as Kincaid roared into her cleavage about himself.

There were a number of high profile guests. She noted the British and French attachés from Munich, their staff, the Italian ambassador and surprisingly Russians - Molotov sitting with Von Ribbentrop's staff - Americans too. A group of businessmen, immaculately attired, were speaking to Speer and Hitler's deputy Rudolf Hess in a discreet huddle. It was the first party Eva had been at where there were no journalists or representatives of the ever-pervasive Propaganda Ministry mingling with the guests.

What she was witnessing was a series of high-level meetings happening sub rosa to the sound of an orchestra.

'Who are those men, Donald?' she enquired, proffering a cigarette to be lit. Kincaid fumbled around his pockets and found a lighter, gold plated with a swastika embossed on it. He cranked it a couple of times, swaying through the booze.

'Those? Bankers, financiers, heads of pharmaceutical companies. We're all looking for a piece of the action. Once Hitler and his boys start taking their Lebensraum, there's going to be a lot of money to be made out of it. I have several of my people here negotiating newsreel, film and publishing rights.'

Kincaid's expression altered momentarily, his eyes glazing over like the night he first spotted her. It was a look of unbridled lust.

She made a note of the men's faces before he took her by the arm to dance. Despite being six sheets to the wind, Kincaid was an accomplished dancer which surprised her.

His moves were assured and she could suddenly see how he was a successful womaniser - rich, funny and charming. She looked back at Unity and Diana. Unity was holding court with several SS junior officers, enjoying their attention. Further back, Diana stared out miserably as Mosley and Joyce leaned in close, drowning their sorrows.

The piece came to an end and everyone applauded in a mannerly fashion. Kincaid turned to Eva, planting a wet whiskey-smelling kiss on her cheek. 'Come to America with me tomorrow. Let me show you around my studios. I could organise a screen test for a motion picture I'm planning to produce.'

Eva was taken aback at the suddenness of the request. She stared into his magnified eyes behind wire lenses, dropped her eyes and, in a voice Madame Yvette would've been proud of, breathed, 'I'd love to.' She then excused herself.

Kincaid was in an ebullient mood, mingling with his associates and filling glasses. Mosley and Diana had left earlier. Diana touched Eva's arm in concern when she told her she'd be flying out to America with Kincaid.

'Don't worry, Diana. I can take care of myself,' Eva assured her with a wink.

Diana hugged her and told her to mind herself and stay in touch.

Unity had met an SS officer and was remaining behind, waving to the three of them that she was in control of the situation. This was indicated with a jolly thumbs-up.

Eva produced her camera, and catching Kincaid's eye, held it up asking would they like to have a photo taken. Never missing an opportunity for his face to be on film, Donald T Kincaid lined up with a group of drunken men who posed for the shot. Pretending to be drunk, Eva tried several times to take the photo to the jeering shouts of the men. Shrugging in apology, she squeezed the shutter just as the group broke apart, the men reeling toward the bar, capturing them perfectly in profile.

Now she had to think of a way to get the camera to Chainbridge before she left for California.

* * *

Diana answered almost immediately after the second knock. Eva whispered into the gap of the hotel door that she was staying at Kincaid's place in Berlin and his car was waiting outside. Eva handed the camera to Diana, telling her she'd dropped it, it had broken and could she drop it into a camera shop in Leicester Square, the address written down on a piece of Kincaid's stationery? The shop would repair it.

'Of course, dear,' whispered Diana. 'Are you sure you're ok?'

'Yes,' grinned Eva. 'He's out cold. How's Oswald?'

'Despondent,' said Diana looking back into the darkened room. She had a careworn air about her but seemed to pull out of it. She turned to Eva. 'You be careful, dear... Promise me?'

Eva touched the delicate hand, marvelling at the length of Diana's finger tips. 'I promise.'

Eva turned and headed back to the car waiting outside.

Oswald flew back to London the following day, his limousine calling by Eva's camera shop. His meeting with Hitler had been brief but unsuccessful. The Reich was not prepared to fund the BUF and Mosley had left empty-handed and out of options.

Unity had remained on as a guest of Eva Braun and Hitler, planning to travel Germany for a few weeks. Diana handed the camera over and the man in the shop coat accepted it with a smile.

Within a few hours, the photograph of Kincaid's associates were sitting on Chainbridge's desk. He spread the photograph and intelligence out across his desk and made phone calls to Kell and Liddle. Looking up at De Witte sitting in the shadows feeding lengths of Braille correspondence through his fingers, he informed them that

Eva had established contact and had photographed a veritable rogues' gallery; including British Nazi sympathisers.

De Witte stopped feeding the intelligence through his fingers momentarily. 'Good.' He started feeding the information again, his face showing no emotion. He was impressed with her.

Eva had developed her friendship with Kincaid through the Goebbels' screen-test reels. It had taken a while, using the auspices of a bogus London casting agent to feed her details through the Hollywood system. Once headshots and film reels were requested, the agent had contacted Berlin.

Kincaid's staff in Burbank, California, saw the reel can with the German Eagle stencilled onto it and jumped at the opportunity. A meeting in New York followed and Kincaid took the bait like a greedy schoolboy.

Chainbridge, along with the F.B.I., had a substantial dossier on him. Kincaid's influence was enormous. Apart from a private film studio in Hollywood, he owned a mansion in Martha's Vineyard and numerous European properties. Although married and a father of nine children, he boasted openly about having several high-profile mistresses.

In Boston circles he had the Chief of Police, the Attorney General and various teamster organisations in 'his pocket'. A fervent anti-communist, he and a number of American anti-communists had arranged functions for Hitler and Mussolini in Berlin in the 1930s. Grandiose with his largesse, he had written large cheques for their fledgling political parties, all in the glare of the media.

This wealth had come allegedly through boot-legging during prohibition. He used this money to help break a Boston longshoremen's strike and take control of the docks. His pay-off from City Hall was under-the-counter and siphoned offshore into various trusts. This money reappeared as armament sales to the Fascists in Spain. He was spotted in Madrid in 1936 along with German 'advisors' shipping in guns, bombs and gold bullion to fund Franco's forces.

His campaign for Mayor of Boston two years earlier ended abruptly after three weeks without explanation. His campaign manifesto used the longshoreman's strike as an example of Communism creeping into 'Freedom-loving America'. Rumours of a young actress overdosing on cocaine at his mansion had clung to him like a smell. Nothing was proved and the story buried, the girl's family dropping a law suit within days of it being issued. The journalist who broke the story was sacked and his card rescinded after pressure from Kincaid's attorneys.

It was this same self-made man that Eva flew with from Berlin to London on a German diplomatic flight, collected by his private chauffeur and stopping at his studio offices near Piccadilly Circus.

Eva remained in the office's reception area as Kincaid presided over several production meetings. She attempted a few times to strike up a conversation with the dour receptionist, a very pretty but disappointed looking brunette. After a while Eva gave up. Glancing around the room, she noted the offices' windows were small. Poor light filtered in on framed photographs of actors and actresses. She spotted the receptionist's head-shot amid them with a hopeful twinkle in her eye.

The other thing she noticed was the phone hardly rang during her time there and the receptionist turned the pages of a magazine slowly, occasionally letting out a sigh. She was no doubt a conquest recently discarded, thought Eva.

By 3pm Kincaid was finished. He swept out into the reception, donning his beige cashmere coat and chomping on a cigar. He barely acknowledged the receptionist who seemed to come to life at the sight of him striding by. 'Let's go, Eva,' he barked. The receptionist almost seemed to slump into her chair in pain.

They descended the stairs, and as she stepped into the limousine, the afternoon bustle of the city was split open by the sound of air-raid sirens. It chilled her to the bone. She had been caught up in a bombing raid by Franco's air force in Valencia in 1937. She flinched involuntarily,

'It's fine, honey, they're just practice drills. Mind you, once Goering throws his bombers at them, we'll be glad we're in California.'

They flew by flying boat from his private jetty at Chelsea Reach along the Thames, banking out over the city; the metropolis flowing below them in a constant motion. Waiting on board for them was a silver service dinner with champagne, American magazines and newspapers.

A young already care-worn male assistant was waiting for Kincaid with documents, among them the schematics of an aeroplane.

Kincaid chuckled when he folded out the aircraft's blueprints. It looked like a warehouse with wings to Eva. She noticed that when he was concentrating, he would produce a golf tee from his jacket pocket and chew on its tapered point. If he was stressed, he would move it around his mouth with his teeth, gnawing on it. If he became furious, it would be hurled at his assistant.

Kincaid authorised by telegram money transfers as down-payments for the aircraft to the tune of ten million dollars. He tipped her a wink as he said it aloud to his assistant. She in turn pretended to be dazzled by this amount, opening her mouth and blinking.

He enjoyed that reaction.

The rest of the flight he was signing off paperwork, contacting his lawyers in Boston via the aircraft's radio, and then putting his long legs up on the facing seat and sleeping. Eva felt a pang of isolation which she decided suited her. She was just a trophy ready for polishing and putting up for display, but otherwise disposable.

She accepted the situation. It gave her the necessary leeway to watch everything and report anything useful. She felt for the receptionist she met a few hours earlier. That girl had probably been sitting on this flight a few months earlier.

The assistant, O'Dowd, went back to the rear seats and sat up writing reports and chewing on a thumb nail the way a dog worries a bone.

They landed in a small cove near Martha's Vineyard which was overlooked by Kincaid's faux-Georgian mansion. The flying boat turned around and departed back to Europe, its vast wings glinting in the morning sunlight.

* * *

It had been two days since they arrived and Eva had exchanged no more than three or four words with Kincaid before they retired to bed. She was standing in the dining room drinking coffee, watching a seal bobbing its head up through the waves. The room had large bay windows that gave a panoramic view of the bay. Apart from a few pleasure yachts further up the cove, the scene probably hadn't changed in millennia.

Her eyes tracked the seal's sleek back as it dipped and slid through the waves like a playful dog. The sun was struggling to penetrate the cloud cover that had parked itself over the cove. Fitful beams shone further out to sea past landfall like veins of a fan; rich blue waves danced like an electric shock over the grey waters.

The mansion was deserted apart from a maid who appeared at random during the day and, to Eva's displeasure, the house was bereft of anything to read. Somewhere in a room upstairs Kincaid's voice boomed out a stream of invectives at some poor minion on the end of a phone. He slammed the phone down with such force she could hear the device clatter off the floor of the room above. She looked around. The room was decorated like an English hunting lodge - heavy curtains, mahogany panelling, various oils depicting fox hunting scenes and an enormous elk's head over a black marble fireplace.

On the mantel piece was a series of framed photographs, children at various ages grinning or frowning with a young Kincaid and plain Shaker-looking Mrs Kincaid. As the family increased in size, she seemed to age at a faster rate than Donald until her last image made her look like an embittered old crone.

A log fire sputtered and spat sparks out and yet seemed incapable of heating the room. She could hear doors banging and the heavy footfall of Kincaid descending the staircase. He strode in and, without breaking his stride, swept her up in his arms planting a kiss on her lips. 'Your screen test is the day after tomorrow.'

They flew into Los Angeles from the bleak North Atlantic weather into the shimmering heat of California. Again, like Martha's Vineyard, she found herself alone, staying in his immense secluded villa overlooking the glittering azure Pacific Ocean. The Philippine staff ignored her and for most of the time she sat on the veranda reading magazines and watching the surf spill over the rocks below to the music on the radio.

Kincaid started his day by quaffing his first shot glass of whiskey and taking her to his private screening room in the basement. To get her up to speed on the role she was being tested for, they watched the first reels of his latest epic about a knight from the court of Richard the Lion Heart taking refuge in a forest and avenging his fall from grace. 'Sounds like Robin Hood,' Eva observed. Kincaid had merely scowled. 'Yeah, well our leading man's a leap ahead of that drunken whoremonger Flynn! '

Kincaid's studios - Liberty Belle Studios off Sunset Boulevard -

were a cavernous warren of sound stages laid out in all manner of guises, South Sea islands, mediaeval castle interiors, an English forest and a Wild West fort. Powerful lights lit up the sets and actors lolled on tables and chairs, smoking or reading scripts, waiting for their cue. Two Sioux Indians, resplendent in war paint, were playing Texas-hold-'em with three knights. The Indians were winning.

This morning was her screen test and despite herself she was nervous. She was being screen tested for the role of a 'plucky handmaid who helps the knight return to favour' – or so the top of her script read.

She was dressed for the part in a shimmering silver gown nipped in tight to her waist with a virgin white wimple framing her perfect cheekbones. The cameraman gave a thumbs-up. Lighting and Make Up made their final adjustments. The director, a rotund man with a horrific greying comb-over, yelled, 'Action!'

Eva immediately slipped into character, taking her naturally husky tone up in pitch and getting some 'pluckiness' into her risible dialogue. The extra, posed where the hero knight would stand, had his back to the shot and openly gawped at her breasts. When she finished her lines, he looked her in the eye and winked.

And that was the end of her test. The lights went off and the sound stages began to hum to the production teams preparing for the days filming.

Kincaid had spent most of his time during the day on the phone in his study, in meetings or hunched over his ticker tape machine. He would turn the air blue with his outbursts should a stock value drop several points. On particularly bad days he would sit sullenly at the dinner table drinking heavily. On more than one morning she would find him sprawled across the table at breakfast in a stupor, clutching ribbons of ticker tape.

Eva was wheeled out when it was party time, which meant every night, dressed in stunning gowns from plush studio wardrobes off set. Her hair and make-up was professionally done by studio staff and she was carefully hidden amid his entourage. In the media glare she would stay three of four paces back from him on the red carpet.

The parties in the villa were wild and Eva, inured to the cabaret life of Germany, was unfazed by the antics of Kincaid and his cronies, the night always ending up with someone overdosing on cocaine or some other substance. Kincaid's personal physician, Dr Harry Gold, would be summoned in the dead of night and either administer a cure or load a body into his car.

Despite his chaotic lifestyle, she always felt safe on Kincaid's arm. He never let her out of his sight when the younger dashing actors milled around her at the parties and, to his credit, could always hold his drink when he had to. She kept her own drinking to a minimum and within a fortnight she had met an intimate circle of men about Kincaid's age. Some were oil men in California here to enjoy the pleasures of starlets; others were clearly military men in civilian clothes and Eva recognised another man from the party in Berlin. He was a large wheezing man, a pharmaceuticals magnate, full of bonhomie with an unbridled lust for skinny actresses. She only caught a glimpse of him coming into the villa and he hadn't seen her.

She didn't catch his name, but Kincaid was in thrall to him and almost a little fearful.

During the long empty afternoons in the mansion, she would write letters to Diana Mosley, knowing full well they would be intercepted and read. Eva, keeping the correspondence as light as possible, would slip in names, descriptions and the status of the men she met. Despite her best efforts, Kincaid refused to give her the name of the big man; he was simply known as 'The Big Fellow'.

Four weeks into her stay, Kincaid burst into her room one morning with a telegram. 'I told you doll, I told you! It's all starting to fall into place. Start packing. We're flying to Berlin tonight!'

Chapter 6

Berchtesgaden 1939: The Kehlsteinhaus

The Tea House sat 183 metres at the top of the Kehlstein mountain, accessed either by the 131 metre elevator bored into the mountain or the specially commissioned road. Hitler chose the road. As the motorcade swept up through the winding tunnels, its progress was observed by Martin Borman and Albert Speer from the sun terrace,

The head of Hitler's security detail strode up, 'He wants to look around.'

'Let's hope he likes it,' said Speer, taking in the view. The clouds danced beneath them around the peak of the nearby Hochter Góll,

'He'd better,' replied Borman, his eyes never leaving the road. 'It cost enough to build.'

The motorcade, all black with red flags fluttering, pulled into the main driveway. Hitler's Mercedes was flanked by SS outriders on powerful motorbikes. Borman rose from leaning against the terrace balcony. They walked through the lavishly decorated main dining area to the reception. An SS honour guard was preparing to greet the entourage. The head of Hitler's personal bodyguard, Schaedle, strode up to them.

Hitler ascended the steps to where Borman, Speer and Goebbels stood waiting in the doorway. The alpine air was refreshing and he stopped to admire the Alps. Removing his fedora, he closed his pale blue eyes, enjoying the sensation of sunlight on his face. He breathed deeply, his throat tingling from the crisp tang of the air. As he started toward the reception, a wave of vertigo swept over him. He steadied himself, inwardly furious that his followers could see this.

Once inside, the Führer marvelled at its craftsmanship. They walked as Speer explained its construction in detail. 'As you can see, mein Führer, from the two windows here in the main dining area you can observe the Watzman and Hochkalter mountains.' They paused to admire the peaks. Speer then guided Hitler through each room, some panelled in rare cembra pine or sand-blasted oak. Hitler was impressed; nodding quietly, stopping, examining, and inquiring, with hands clasped firmly behind his back when he wasn't shaking the hands of each of his household staff, beaming and joking awkwardly in the main reception area.

Then he was ushered to his private chamber off the main dining room. Speer's scaled model of New Berlin, moulded according to Hitler's vision, almost filled the entire room. Hitler leaned into it closely, holding his breath in wonder.

Das Museum von gebesiegt - The Museum of the Vanquished - caught his eye and made him smile. He envisioned the British Crown Jewels, French Impressionist works, Fabergé eggs and Mozart's manuscripts. And in pride of place, Lenin's mausoleum.

'Perhaps,' Goebbels suggested, 'Stalin's head in a jar of formaldehyde or mounted like a hunter's trophy?' They all roared with laughter.

The rest of the guests arrived and the four men left the room to attend Hitler's 50th birthday party. Goebbels paused, looking back at the model citadel. Eradicating Communism was a personal crusade for Hitler; what if they managed to snatch Lenin's body sooner rather than later? It would be a sensational bargaining chip. He began to hatch a plot, an idea so brazen that, if it was pulled off, it would change the world. But before that could happen, there would have to be a war.

The following morning, Himmler drove directly to his new headquarters in Berlin, SS Hauptampt. The city had a freshness to it he hadn't noticed before. The population moved about their business around the thriving Potsdamer Platz, the façades gleaming and the skies a cloudless blue. Everywhere around the capital gave the sense of success and order. He nestled himself deeper into the leather depths of his seat.

Across from him were two Waffen SS: General Rolf Metzger and a young impossibly beautiful Aryan Captain, Thor Schenker. All three were perusing a manila folder stamped at the highest level of confidentiality.

Metzger's grey-steel eyes twinkled as he completed his review. 'If this goes wrong, Reichsführer .... '

Himmler's eyes narrowed behind his wire frame glasses, a faint smile danced around his lips, making his moustache twitch.

'This is why we selected you, General. It won't go wrong,'

Schenker's head snapped up. It reminded Himmler of an obedient

Doberman. He found he was unable to look away from this Adonis. Hitler was right; this boy was a prime specimen.

'I can't foresee any problems.' His cultured accent and his refined sense of dress confirmed he was born to wear the uniform. Himmler felt himself dumpy in this beautiful boy's presence. He tried to concentrate on the dossier. He tried not to blush.

Metzger lit a cigarette. Himmler tried to wave the smoke away with a tailored leather glove.

'My concern is that we get a local policeman who just happens to be thorough.'

Himmler afforded himself a small smile as the limousine turned off Prince Albrecht Strasse down into a cavernous parking lot below the SS Hauptamt building.

'The nature of this will be so heinous that the Gestapo, Waffen SS and Diplomatic corps will want it. It is imperative that we execute this plan efficiently to forward the Führer's plan.'

The limousine pulled up alongside an army truck painted in a gun-metal grey, the number plates and registration erased. Metzger and Schenker alighted and, with Himmler, strode to the rear of the truck. Pulling the tarpaulin window aside, a group of soldiers acknowledged the three of them with the briefest of nods. All looked like hardened street fighters, Metzger's personal detail.

'Excellent,' said Metzger.

Himmler touched his elbow and whispered into his ear, 'If you pull this off, General, I can promise you a most excellent theatre of operations,'

Schenker whistled slowly, and began to follow the General's lead. His smile almost stretched his jaw.

* * *

It was the dogs barking in the yard that woke farmer Rupert Lowe. He reached for his glasses and sat upright in the bed. The vast bulk of his wife Gertrude shifted and groaned as she tried to settle into a more comfortable position. He stared into the darkness, the window shutters rattling slightly again, the barking, then a shrill cry from one of the hounds. A quick succession of whinnies, shrill barks and cries rang out, then silence.

Lowe slipped out of the bed, his feet dancing on the cold floor. His stomach churned in fear. He could hear movement outside. The farm was two miles away from the Polish border and there had been reports of strange occurrences over the past few days. In two nearby farms, machinery had been vandalised in the night, some buildings had also been subjected to arson. The tension between the two countries was beginning to spill into the countryside. At the market last weekend a row had broken out between two German and Polish families who for years had traded amicably. The Gestapo had appeared out of nowhere, broken it up, and forcibly beaten the Polish family across the border.

Lowe loaded his shotgun quietly. His daughters Lottie, Dorothy and Anna peeked out at their father from their loft bed. Lowe raised his finger to shush them and went down the staircase he had built and installed a month after his wedding, fifty years ago. He opened the front door and spread his still broad form across the threshold, gun raised. He kept all the lights off, allowing his eyes to adjust to the gloom quickly.

Two figures scampered across between the barn and his tool shed.

'Who's there?' he shouted out into the darkness. He was met with silence.

Then a sudden movement in his peripheral vision made him turn. He fired the shotgun's double-barrels into the night, the report booming. His dogs should have been raising hell by now.

Then he heard automatic machine gun fire. His legs buckled beneath him, white hot light flashed, consuming his vision, and a sweat drenched his nightshirt, mingling with his blood. He tried to rise up but was kicked back by a man in army fatigues whose design he didn't recognise. The man looked mature, grey haired with cold grey eyes. He pointed a pistol into Lowe's forehead. The last thing Lowe saw was the man smiling. It was a warm smile as he pulled the trigger. Faintly in the distance, Lowe could hear his daughters screaming.

Metzger made his way up into the loft where the three women huddled. Wiping his brow, he smiled at his incredible good fortune. How did the saying go? 'Country girls, country appetites'. He vaulted into the bed, brandishing a bayonet. 'Now ladies, who's first?'

Schenker moved through the house while Metzger and the other ten SS entertained themselves up in the girls' loft. His heart was racing with the excitement; the hapless farmer having been his second ever kill. He moved through the kitchen and came suddenly upon the crouching form of the dead farmer's wife. Gertrude launched herself at him, a vast nightgown swooping toward him with a banshee howl. She flattened him onto the cold floor, his head striking the stone tiles making him see stars. She straddled him, he couldn't breathe, she produced a huge carving knife from her sleeve and, deftly changing hands, flipped the blade toward him.

He wrestled his Luger free from its holster and fired point blank. Gertrude's head flipped back, spraying blood all over him, the walls and the ceiling before she collapsed forward, her dead weight pressing like a vice on his lungs.

He lay there for minutes, his breath coming in short gasps. He thought about his strict catholic upbringing in Bavaria, the nuns, the mystery of the sacraments and his gift, his trick. As a child he liked to maim little animals. Starting with insects, he quickly moved onto feral kittens, birds and mice in the privacy of his room. He'd derived exquisite pleasure in baiting and torturing the neighbour's dachshund that had annoyed him. He had tricked the noisy little bastard into his family's barn and fixed a leash to its neck, the other end wrapped around the steel leg of his father's work bench. He set to work on it with the knives from the cook's pantry. He found it hard not to rush to the finale and learned over the years how to drag out the exquisite torture.

After each of these animals had been slain, little Thor would extend out his arms like the saviour and pray for these poor animals' souls and he would bury them guiltily under his mother's rose bushes when left alone with his aged nanny.

This gift he brought to the SA, then the SS. His rigorous attention to detail during the Kristallnacht brought him to Himmler's attention. He believed from an early age he had the power to grant life or death, that he was in effect the hand of God.

This gift he had bestowed on the elderly shopkeeper who had come out protecting his shop front from Schenker's charges. Schenker had shot him in the head, citing self-defence. The man was armed only with a sweeping brush hurling insults in Yiddish. That night Schenker had found his calling, inspired by the words of Hitler, taking Goebbels propaganda as Gospel, an avenging angel of death for the Reich. The people rounded up that night were handed over for him and his cohorts to interrogate. In the police cells in the wee hours of the morning, Schenker's skills were honed. These thoughts floated around as the vast expanse of Gertrude expired, slumping and pushing him harder against the floor.

Her blood was flowing in thick bursts onto him. He was going to be found dead under this woman. He started to scream for help. His voice was lost in the screams of the girls above. Eventually Metzger's head appeared amid the woman's blood-matted hair. Looking at Schenker he called back to the troop behind him, 'Looks like he's finally popped his cherry.' Amid the laughter, Gertrude was hauled off him and he gasped the air around him.

An army radio barked into life on the kitchen table. For a radius of two miles, Metzger's forces were attacking local German farms.

Somewhere in the distance a farm was being torched, the horizon beginning to glow from the blaze. Schenker rose unsteadily to his feet, smelling like a butcher's block.

Metzger was covered in blood, his men also. They had a sweaty high coming off them; they were all panting like hounds. Schenker retched onto the floor and onto his highly polished boots.

Metzger looked at him in disdain. 'Christ, Schenker, pull yourself together.'

He picked up Schenker's Luger and handed it to one of the younger men. The soldier looked at it in puzzlement until Metzger, reaching down, picked up the carving knife on the floor and plunged it to the hilt into the soldier's chest. Pulling the stunned man closer onto the blade, he twisted it repeatedly, then threw the soldier onto the floor. The rest of the men stood stunned.

Metzger turned to them. 'He will receive a funeral you could only dream of. He will join the great fallen German soldiers who are about the shed their life's blood for the Reich. Remember him well, gentlemen. He is a hero.'

He then pulled documentation from his tunic, drenched in blood, and checked the photograph on it. Satisfied that it matched the man he had just stabbed, he placed the documents into the dying soldier's tunic.

They headed out into the courtyard.

Metzger turned to Schenker. 'Torch the outbuildings, leave the farmhouse standing.' Schenker, recovering his composure, saluted straight-armed. Metzger spoke slowly, 'Leave the farmhouse standing.' Metzger prayed this idiot wouldn't be drafted to his units when the battles proper started.

The following morning, the local constabulary made their way between the ravaged farms. Lowe's farm was the worst the district investigator had ever had to deal with. His men were traumatised and stood in huddles in the courtyard smoking and whispering.

The dogs had had their throats cut and had been eviscerated with some kind of large knife. Their entrails were strewn around the yard. The farmer's body had been dumped in the well; he was like a rag doll as they hoisted him up onto the ground. The outer buildings had been burnt down, the livestock slaughtered with automatic weapons. Spent casings lay scattered everywhere.

The girls loft though was nothing like anything they had ever seen. The pathologist arrived with his team from Berlin, then the Gestapo, police and representatives of the Führer, followed by the press. Cars began to block up the roadway, interfering with the investigation.

Then officials from the Propaganda Ministry arrived.

Whatever evidence was around was now utterly contaminated as film cameras were set up and mounted, and Gestapo operatives took photographs.

The investigator saluted the Gestapo plain clothes officers smartly. It was an honour to have these men come all the way from Berlin. He led the two men into the kitchen. Tables and chairs lay overturned and there, in the middle of the room, the immense bulk of Gertrude lay. Beside her lay a man with a carving knife buried up to its hilt in his chest. The man was wearing a Polish Officer's uniform. Documentation showed he was Polish Army.

'Looks like the old bird got one,' said the investigator, lighting up a cigarette. It killed the smell, but only just.

The Gestapo men looked around, taking everything in. Two SS stepped in and stood alongside them, summoning the investigator over. He stood, slightly stooped, fidgeting with his hat, clearly out of his depth.

'Thank you for your assistance and prompt request for us. We will handle this awful incident from here on. Please submit all your findings directly to me,'

The investigator was handed a card listing the address as Himmler's headquarters in Berlin. They saluted and the investigator responded after a pause. He hadn't contacted any Gestapo; he'd only got the call himself a few hours earlier.

The Polish Ambassador to Germany, Jozeph Lipski, re-read Von Ribbentrop's communiqué. After initial diplomatic success and high level discussions with the Axis powers, Lipski was now completely isolated. For months he had been trying to meet Von Ribbentrop face-to-face, only to be rebuffed at every diplomatic level, the same with Molotov in Moscow. Both nations were behaving as if his country didn't even exist. The Italians had promised to assist, but so far nothing from them either. The British and French were making enquiries on Poland's behalf with equally limited success. Every newspaper, newsreel and radio broadcast reported on Molotov, Von Ribbentropp, Chamberlain, Mussolini and Hitler ad nauseum. Lipski

103

occasionally appeared in newsreels, receiving column inches in the newspapers, but was never mentioned in the film commentaries.

The Polish government, fearful of Germany regaining territories ceded after Versailles, had despatched cavalry columns to the disputed regions. Horse cavalry and bicycle-mounted troops, bows and arrows against the coming lightening. The country was put on a war footing and had its embassies in friendly countries discreetly looking for assurances of support. The communiqué in Lipski's hand was stamped 'strictly confidential'. Polish Special Forces had been caught slipping over the border and attacking peaceful neighbouring German farms. He skimmed through the rhetoric to the final sentence which stated, 'Any further attacks will be considered a hostile act of a nation state and will be dealt with accordingly.' Attached were facsimiles of identity documents found on a dead Polish officer, killed during an attack on a farm. With the communiqués was a package containing film footage and forensic photographs taken at the Lowe farm by the Propaganda Ministry,

Lipski watched them in revulsion. As a footnote, the ammunition retrieved was from British-issue machine guns. Were British commandos operating with these men? Was Poland deliberately precipitating a crisis in the hope of dragging England into an avoidable conflict? Lipski began making a series of phone calls. The first was to the Polish Army Command. Who the hell was this man whose the identity papers had were being cited?

In London, Chainbridge, Liddell and Kell reviewed the recent dispatches with a sense of impending doom. The Polish army attacking peaceful German villagers with British supplied weapons, Thompson M1928s to be precise, according to the dispatch lying on the table in front of them. Also, a communications tower in Germany had been attacked by Polish special Special Forces, though verification was sketchy.

The German High Command was preparing a dossier. According to the embassy in Warsaw, German tanks and heavy Panzer divisions had been spotted moving toward the Polish border. The German war machine was now springing into life despite reassurances to the contrary from Von Ribbbentropp and Hitler. They were being deployed to specific regions to protect the Germans living close to the Polish border, Berlin was now telling the world.

'Panzers, motorised divisions and Luftwaffe support to protect a couple of dairy farmers, that doesn't quite add up,' observed Kell dryly.

The room was heavy with cigarette smoke and, beyond, a beautiful summer's day tried vainly to get through the window pane. There was nothing from the Moscow bureau about any evacuation plan, though armament production was shifting up a gear.

Lipski had sent several 'eyes only' level messages concerning the German accusations to the governments of England and France. There had been absolutely no Polish forces anywhere near the German border, but now they were mobilising army and cavalry units in response to Germany's manoeuvres. The German's weren't responding at all, a wall of silence descending around Berlin.

Chainbridge peered over the edge of his glasses. 'It appears,

Gentlemen, we are on the brink of war.'

'Hitler's a master of brinkmanship,' countered Kell, the unease carrying through his voice as if he didn't really believe what he was saying.

'Could be sabre-rattling, looking for more concessions. It's the Foreign Office and our French counterparts' desire that we keep Hitler and Stalin at each other's throats. The Foreign Office believes that Hitler will more than likely strike east, whatever pact those two lunatics have struck,'

Chainbridge held his gaze, 'Hitler wants a war, it's as simple as that, and he sees us as the biggest threat to his ambitions. We've committed to defending Poland, should he invade. He's going to invade.'

'Stalin?' Kell toyed absently with his glasses as he spoke and continued sipping the cold dregs from the tea cup. The room began to feel stifling in the summer heat.

'Poland is about to become the first acquisition of Russia's 'Near abroad'. Stalin's keen to start expanding the revolution.' De Witte had an operative in Moscow who had confirmed that the Soviet Union was moving large numbers of armoured columns and troops to Poland's borders. Molotov and Stalin were using the term 'a zone of privileged interest' when referring to Poland and, glancing at the map, that could also encompass Estonia, Latvia, Lithuania and Finland.

On Chainbridge's advice, the British Government had beefed up its security at its embassy in Helsinki after the peace negotiations between Finland and Russia. Should Russia invade again, which was becoming more likely, this would give Stalin a toehold in the Scandinavian countries. The problem politically was that Finland was friendly with Germany. If England went to war with Germany, the embassy was vulnerable with its small garrison.

Chainbridge lit up from the stub of a previous cigarette. It wasn't Hitler he was worrying about now, it was Stalin. 'We have intelligence out of Moscow that the army's 'on manoeuvres' on her borders with Poland. The bear has woken up.'

A pall hung in the room. The second part of the intelligence was that the rail link to Tyumen had been completed and Gulag labour in the Urals had increased two-fold. Again nothing concrete, but it appeared that some heavy manufacturing equipment was moving toward the Urals which suggested they were preparing for war.

'I'll inform the Prime Minister and I'll contact the Army, see if any of the arsenals have been compromised. We probably sold those bloody guns to the Poles anyway.'

Kell rose, his demeanour deflated. He left, leaving Liddle and Chainbridge to their thoughts. Chainbridge had to get news to Eva in Berlin.

In Krakow, Warsaw and all the major cities, the intelligentsia were being listed by the Gestapo and dossiers were being created on them. Henk Molenaar's name was already included. German spies were preparing the groundwork for invasion. British and French spies were feeding the information back in the hope of keeping things in check.

Chainbridge picked up the phone and asked the operator to find the hotel in Berlin where Donald T Kincaid was staying. Then he contacted De Witte who was in Cambridge sourcing new intelligence operatives, instructing him to return to London immediately.

He returned to his chambers where Meenagh awaited him. His drive through the London rush hour was a hot, uncomfortable ride. The late summer heat was oppressive and the rank smell of the Thames permeated the air. In the gridlock he watched the people walking, wrapped up in their daily lives. Mothers, babies and toddlers mingled with a stream of business men in bowler hats. They flowed across the bridges of London from Threadneedle Street, a uniform sea of black and white, giving a sense of stability and security. The gloom had broken to reveal a beautiful late summer evening, he thought as he stepped through the front door of his chambers. For the first time in years, Meenagh saw her husband visibly depressed. As always, he lightened up as she stepped toward him, eyes lowered, arms open in welcome. He ran his fingers through her greying hair and kissed her. They retreated to his study and he put a shellac disc onto the turntable.

As Mozart's Piano Sonata Number 11 hissed and crackled through the speakers, they held each other tightly, with the same intensity as the night they had met in Bombay ten years previously.

* * *

The restaurant off the Potsdam Plaza was exclusive to high

ranking Nazi party members. Kincaid was mingling with Goebbels, his wife Magda, and their 'dear friend' Eva Braun. Hitler was unable to attend, excusing himself with a migraine. Bormann was at another table and, nearby, the erudite Speer was holding court, discussing architecture and other topics close to an aesthete's heart.

Eva Braun was light hearted tonight. She had laughed in a sisterly fashion, observing that there were now two Evas at the table, referring to Eva Molenaar as the second. Goebbels remarked at how beautiful they both looked as he assembled a champagne glass tower and filled it with expensive champagne, creating a waterfall effect from the top glass down. Kincaid, squeezing Eva closer to him, said she was going to be a great star of the silver screen. The table toasted her. All around, the revellers were almost frenzied in their enjoyment of the cabaret, the room a sea of black uniforms, leather webbing and scarlet armbands.

Eva left the dinner party, excusing herself after a waitress had whispered an urgent message into her ear. In the restrooms, an attendant handed a slip of paper punched in Braille point. The pit of her stomach gripped in fear - her grandfather's name was on the list of targeted intellectuals. The attendant offered her a cigarette and set light to the message for her at the same time, flushing the ashes down the toilet. Eva thanked the girl and tipped her before leaving.

She came back to the table where Goebbels was laughing. 'Did I miss something?' she asked smiling,

Kincaid rubbed his hands together in a sudden burst of hilarity. The gesture made the rasping sound characteristic of calloused hands, the hands of a labourer.

'We're just talking here. Seems that the tanks are goin' to roll any day soon. It's as we say in my part of the world – "It's a slam dunk!" – the Polacks and Brits won't know what hit them!'

The table reduced to laughter as Goebbels repeated, 'Slam Dunk! Ja! - slam dunk!'

Eva laughed along with them, tears of anguish only just held back. The darkness that had haunted her peripheral vision for years seemed to close in further. She could hear Kincaid shouting over the din of the party as he rose with a champagne glass raised, 'Heil Hitler!'

The club, taking his cue, all rose and chanted it. Eva Braun, Goebbels and his wife were crying tears of euphoria. The voices rose to the rhythmic chant and the band stamped and struck out a beat. Eva's thoughts were of her grandfather and De Witte, and for a split second she thought she saw Jonas moving through the crowd. He drew nearer and Eva's heart began to race, but the vision passed and the man she thought was Jonas turned out to be a waiter.

Leaving the party telling Kincaid she felt unwell, she returned to the hotel floor reserved for special guests of the Propaganda Ministry. Kincaid had been given access in Berlin to an immense penthouse suite fitted with several phone lines allowing him access to his various interests in America. It wasn't as homely as the mansion in Martha's Vineyard, but she judged that she had a better chance of uncovering some intelligence here as his guard was down amid his Nazi companions. It had taken nearly a year for him to

110

accept her and their relationship as she gradually built up his trust.

Kincaid didn't returned that night and, with the apartment empty, it gave Eva a chance to slip into the study where Kincaid spent most of his time. It had two clocks on the wall, one set to German time, the other indicating the time on the West Coast of the USA, an eight hour difference, meaning Kincaid spent between 4pm and anywhere close to midnight here in this study most days. The room was lushly furbished with comfortable black leather settees, large enough for Kincaid to stretch out on, chairs and a sturdy plain writing desk. There was a large silver screen which could be pulled down from the ceiling and, opposite, an alcove containing a film projector. A stack of film reels were placed in a cabinet, the two stacks marked 'WIP' or 'Fin'.

Pinned up on the walls of the room were various drafts of posters for movies and promotional literature. On the desk was a tidy pile of scripts at various draft stages, a pen and ink set in silver of an Eagle, and a half-empty bottle of Jameson whiskey. One drawer in his desk was locked, the key attached to the chain of his pocket watch. Eva removed two hairpins from her hair and forced the lock deftly.

She flipped through the various documents and envelopes - nothing. Then, as she was closing the drawer, it caught on something. Running her hand under it, she felt an envelope. She removed the drawer carefully and, stacking its contents on the desk, turned it over. The envelope was fixed to the base with glue. She opened it, running a finger nail beneath the flap. Instinctively she paused, frozen, listening for the tell-tale click of his key in the front door.

She held her breath and opened her mouth, fractionally improving her hearing. Silence.

In the envelope was a communiqué between Hitler, Himmler and Goering to Kincaid's studios. It was an itemized bill for Kincaid's services. Eva flattened it out and read it carefully. It totalled to nearly a million dollars. She ran into her private quarters, grabbed her box brownie and took photographs of the flattened sheet. She replaced everything as she found it, sliding the drawer back. She gave a cursory glance around, double-checking that nothing looked untoward.

She left through the bustling foyer and walked to the central train station. From Berlin Central she paid for her ticket in cash, giving a good, but not ostentatious, tip to ensure she had a private sleeping berth for the five hundred and thirty five miles to Krakow. Kincaid was by nature generous and she had a sizeable amount of dollars at her disposal without his asking questions as to how she spent it.

Over the past few months, he had schemed and promoted a heavy weight boxing match in Berlin with newsreel rights exclusively for the American market. German heavyweight champion Max Schmeling versus Joe Louis at the Berlin Olympic Stadium; billed 'The Battle of the Bombers'. He'd negotiated a huge amount of advance money from the American networks for the rights and film reels to be produced by Goebbels' Propaganda Ministry.

Ticket sales sold the Stadium out for an event which Kincaid knew full well would never transpire. After Jesse Owens had won a gold medal at the 1936 Olympic Games, Hitler was cagey about having coloureds beating white German athletes in sporting events. Under his pressure, the plug was pulled on the whole thing and everyone walked away with a sizeable profit, only the backers and fans getting stung.

Kincaid had pulled a similar stunt in the early 1930s in New Jersey and had to flee for his life, breaking speed limits through the turnpike running from the mob. After that, he always carried a gun, a Smith and Wesson, in a shoulder holster.

From this latest scam, Kincaid had handed Eva a bundle of US dollars to do with whatever she wanted which she had used to secure a berth on a ship departing Gdansk for Southampton for her grandfather and immediate family under the name of De Witte. Then she had obtained travel permits for them from the German underground which had formed once Hitler had taken power.

These perfectly forged papers had been paid for in cash by her and arranged for collection in one of the deposit boxes in the station. The key was slipped to her as she purchased her rail ticket by a female underground operative standing in the queue beside her.

Checking in her compact to ensure she wasn't being followed, Eva went to the line of boxes and quickly found the locker. She removed the permits, ensuring her black fur stole and hat covered her face. In their place she left the brownie camera and four reels of Braille correspondence concerning her recent meetings. In the ladies toilets she handed the key back to the operative who was pouting into a mirror re-adjusting her make-up.

Before she boarded the train, Eva placed the hat and stole in a refuse bin. From her handbag she produced a beret and brightly coloured neck scarf, making sure she mixed with porters, milling passengers and the clouds of steam billowing from the locomotive. Once settled into her compartment, she began to relax momentarily. She tipped the steward, ensuring she was not to be disturbed, and showed him her racial papers with Goebbels' stamp on them. He saluted straight-armed and promised her a peaceful journey, thrilled to be dealing with someone so close to the Reich's most powerful men. It was an early morning departure and not fully booked, mostly businessmen reading newspapers, but worryingly with a few SS, Gestapo and German Army officers dotted about the aisles.

On more than one occasion she was stopped in the Pullman lounge and her papers requested with a polite smile. Once they saw Goebbels signature clearing her racial status, they blanched and moved on from her with the briefest of salutes.

She sat alone at a pre-reserved table in the dining car and smoked, watching the countryside slip by, drinking coffee and reflecting. As the German countryside transformed into the Polish countryside, she watched the shimmering sunset across the fields and farms, glinting off farm machinery, buildings, streams and lakes. Whole communities passed her, some stopping from their labours to watch the steam train rush clattering past them.

She retired to bed. Beneath her pillow she kept a small thin stiletto in its sheath. Also, as a precaution, she jammed her overnight bag against the door. Being a light sleeper it would give her time to react if someone was to try to force the door.

Her grandfather's house looked derelict, the façade and gardens in poor repair. She realised she hadn't been home in two years. The neighbouring houses were pristine but his house itself reflected the demeanour of its occupant. Henk Molenaar shuffled to the door and opened it. Eva was taken aback. Her once tall, robust grandfather was now stooped and bedraggled. She could smell a blend of body odour, tobacco and whiskey upon him.

'Oh Dziadzio,' she whispered as he held out his arms. His bones seemed to be pushing out through his skin, his shirt and his cardigan. He summoned a smile from inside his beard. 'Eva, my dear, what a surprise.' His voice was a rasping whisper. 'I was about to make some coffee.'

She guided him into the kitchen where unwashed pots, pans and crockery lay strewn across the counters and sink. He lit a cigarette, a racking cough arising from his lungs. Absently he spat on the floor. Agneska would have given him a reproachful look, but her absence was felt throughout the house.

Eva felt immense guilt for not having attended the funeral six months earlier while she tried to remain a cold dispassionate spy. Old cobwebs hung from window panes. The curtains had remained open since the funeral, and the windows were grimy. Henk had grown a beard in mourning. It sat about his face and chest unevenly, stained with tobacco around the mouth and nostrils. In the afternoon light, his skin looked seer, his eyes white balls with pinprick irises.

Opening every window, Eva cleaned the kitchen, swept the stone floor, and washed and laundered every piece of clothing and bedding. Then she ran a bath and tenderly bathed the old man, letting him sleep as she sat by the bed, reading to him and holding his hand. In the fading light, he seemed transparent on the pillow. She thought she could detect its intricate lacework beneath his features as his breathing came in short gasps.

'Why didn't you contact me, Grampy?' she whispered, but understood after Aga's death he had ceased living, enduring a lingering death that was taking longer than expected. Talking to neighbours, they told her that he rebuffed them at every opportunity. They eyed her suspiciously, this beautiful woman abandoning her family, her blood, then reappearing near the old man's death.

She had organised to meet her cousins in St Mary's Basilica in Krakow that afternoon, so she wrapped herself in Aga's old great coat. It was dusty and still carried about it the faintest whiff of her favourite scent. A wave of nostalgia brought a smile to her face as she arranged a headscarf about her head and caught the bus to the city.

The Basilica's interior shimmered in the candlelight. An organ was playing quietly, its mellifluous sounds echoing about the vaulted ceiling. Eva recognised the piece as being by Bach as she spied her two cousins - both girls - Michaela and Silvia - peeping out beneath modest shawls kneeling in pews in the shadows just off the main apse.

Eva genuflected for the first time in years in front of Wit Stowsz's

116

grand altar, reflecting on whether there was a place for someone like her in heaven, before slipping in beside them without making eye contact. The altar was quiet, the host covered, and the altar boys and deans went about their solemn duties. There were a few people sitting and kneeling in afternoon meditation, mostly elderly, though, possibly parents praying to God in whispered prayers for their children's future.

Eva quickly explained her plan to the girls. They were to leave the day after next and get themselves and their families to Gdansk and on to England. She handed over the documentation. Silvia noted they had the stamp of the German Eagle. Eva told them that the invasion was imminent. No-one was going to question these papers once the shooting started,

'What about Grandpa?' Eva asked, mindful that they were the only ones in the pews within earshot. Still she pitched her voice to the lowest whisper, looking furtively around. She thought she saw the figure of a man slip back into the shadows behind them.

'He's turned everyone's help down,' whispered Michaela. A strand of pure blonde hair fell over her eye and she angled her head so it would fall away, Eva thought she was a real beauty, a heart-breaker.

'I'll help him then. You two go. Go now and do not talk to anyone. Good luck.' She kissed them both and left them without looking back. As she reached the last pew, she genuflected again, looking up at the cross and the exquisite stained glass windows, and asking God for the strength to endure the years to come.

Peering through the gloom, she could no longer see the girls and assumed they had slipped out through another door. She paused, checking and re-checking that no one had followed her, then left as silently as a ghost, walking through the market square, head down, scarf pulled tight about her, avoiding any eye contact.

No one seemed to realise what was going to happen, what horrors were about to befall them should Germany invade their country.

The stall holders were breaking down their pitches for the night and the square was beginning to clear. Eva felt as if she was a modern-day Cassandra and prayed to God that her family would believe her.

As she left she heard the mournful bugle call of the Hejnal from the Basilica. It was a sound she heard every night in her dreams, and would continue to do so until her dying day.

The house was quiet when she entered. She called out her grandfather's name and made her way through every room searching for him. No lights were on. The old floorboards creaked under her steps as she ascended the staircase. The library was the last room past the bedrooms and a light shone underneath it. She looked in.

Henk Molenaar lay slumped at his desk, the lamplight washing his features white. Eva touched his arm and found it cold, she felt for a pulse in his neck and his wrist. Nothing. He was dead.

Eva gently kissed his cheeks and said her goodbyes, running her fingers through his hair. These past days it had regained its old sheen and texture. It felt like the hair of young man. He was smiling peacefully and his arm was held out across the desk, the fingers coiled as if holding someone else's hand.

Eva climbed the ladder that swung across the shelves to the volume she was seeking. It was a large Bible, sturdily bound with a heavy hide cover and an extremely valuable illuminated codex. Henk had told her it was an original Coptic Bible, possibly first century Roman, almost priceless. Moving about the house and through Henk's writing desk, she located the house deeds. Every legal document was placed between the Bible's perfect ancient pages. She located his cashbox and removed all of the bank notes. She then went through Aga's dusty unopened jewellery box. She found a diamond ring, and several gold bracelets and pearls. She put them all on, covering them with her dress.

Discovering her old bicycle, she rode to the train station, leaving the dead man behind in his favourite place. A man who had once gotten drunk with Rimbaud in Paris, fenced with Ezra Pound and debated with Freud was now at peace. At his favourite writing desk, he was holding his beloved Aga's hand surrounded by his treasured tomes.

Eva was grieving, but she couldn't show it. Her life as she had known it was gone. it was a sensation she couldn't shake. As the train hurtled overnight toward Berlin, she said goodbye to Krakow and Warsaw, to Poland, and to the ghosts of Henk, Aga and Jonas. Absently, her thoughts drifted to Theo. Had he ever become the artist he had aspired to be?

Her conscience juggled the fact that she was saving lives but losing her very essence. Tomorrow she would drape herself in the finery that Donald T Kincaid would lavish on her. She would dine, drink and dance with the men who were engineering a war. There were plenty of girls like her, pretty little moths drawn to the flame of power, basking in its dangerous rays and loving every moment of it.

When she arrived in Berlin, she purchased sturdy brown paper. Wrapping the bible in it with the valuable documents between its pages, Eva took it to a bookstore off the Potsdam Plaza.

Amid the lines of books she found the clerk; Hugh O'Connor, an Irish friend of Chainbridges. She handed him the parcel, giving him the code word 'Tome'. He took it and smiled. He'd have it sent to Chainbridge's shop immediately.

One week later, at 4.45 am on Friday September the 1st 1939, the guns of the German battleship Schleswig-Holstein opened fire on the city of Gdansk on Hitler's orders. The warship was stationed in the harbour, supposedly on a good-will visit and rained down its shells upon the population indiscriminately whereupon German Army Group North, under the command of General Von Bock, and Germany Army Group South under the command of General Von Rundstedt, commenced the invasion.

Two days later, the United Kingdom, its Commonwealth countries and France declared war on Germany. Seventeen days later, Generals Kovalev and Timoshenko poured their armoured divisions into Poland from the Russian borders. The speed of the German advance had caught everyone by surprise, and Stalin didn't want to be left behind.

The British and French had estimated that Poland could hold out for two months, giving them time to prepare assistance. The invasion by Germany and Russia from the North, South and West, committed two million men against the Polish army numbering only 950,000.

The invaders captured every moment on film. Night after night the cinemas screened the newsreels across Germany. Eva would sit with Kincaid as the martial marching music and belligerent commentary boomed out. The audience around them would cheer and applaud at the images of their soldiers, their tanks and their fighter aircraft. These scenes would jump-cut to Hitler reviewing the progress of the invasion with his generals and sweeping his arm across maps of Poland, appearing to make brilliant decisions.

Eva flinched with every shell fired from German 88s, followed by the thick blooming explosions of Polish soil. Within a fortnight, the Polish Army had been routed once the Luftwaffe had gained air superiority. The film reels in the cinemas now showed the German armoured divisions driving through the streets of Warsaw, cutting to bombers' sights dropping their payloads onto the cities below. Eva lost contact with her cousins, all communications cut by the invasion. Then word filtered back from Gdansk that people boarding ferries were being turned away as German warships and U-Boats were now blockading the harbour and the seas around the coast. Her family never made it to the ships outward bound to England.

* * *

Thor Schenker sat nervously waiting for his meeting with Himmler. He noted that over Himmler's door was a sign that read 'No Jews Are Welcome Here'. Three motorised Waffen SS divisions had left without him for Poland under Metzger's command. The SS headquarters were moving at a different pace now; communications were a constant stream, the staff going about their duties in terse silence. After the Lowe farm, he and Metzger had attacked two more isolated farm houses, repeating the massacre and ensuring that the Gestapo was involved.

Schenker had done better on these subsequent occasions. Instead of killing an old lady, he had come up against someone nearer his own age. The boy, no more than eighteen, had surprised him in a barn, brandishing a scythe. Schenker, in a panic, fired off a round before the Thompson's breech jammed, the bullets missing the boy. They wrestled to the ground, grunting, gouging and punching, the machine gun becoming wedged under Schenker's back. The rising dust had made Schenker's wind pipe contract so that he wheezed throughout the struggle. With tears clouding his vision, he fought with all of his strength, managing to roll on top of the boy, the muscles in his arms twitching with the strain. He looked momentarily down at him, the mouth twisted back revealing perfect white teeth, the hair tousled. He wrenched the scythe away when the boy, distracted, twisted his head up at the sounds of machine gun fire outside, and buried it into the boy's chest repeatedly.

Breathless he looked into his dying victim's eyes, rose up onto his knees and, head tilted back, commended his soul to the almighty.

Running his fingers gently through the boy's hair, Schenker bent down and kissed him on his lips stained with blood. The sensation of that moment came back to him every time he replayed the scene in his mind.

His thoughts were broken as he was summoned into the office. Himmler was standing looking out at Berlin's skyline. He spun on his heel as Schenker entered. The blond hair was shorn tight. Himmler thought, why did he shed those beautiful tresses?

'Sit down, Captain.' Himmler indicated a leather chair in front of his desk.

He studied the young man, his poise, the ease of youth as he strode across the room. Schenker's personal file lay open on his desk; three generations of Aryan blood verified on both sides of the family, excellent health and loyal party member. Risen through the ranks of the SA as a teenager, informing on the officers targeted during the 'Night of the Long Knives' and then rising meteorically through the ranks of the Waffen SS.

He had distinguished himself during the Kristallnacht pogrom, co-ordinating and commanding attacks on the Jewish mercantile zones. He had displayed a ruthless streak during this operation, dispatching an eighty year old man with a Luger; this action led to him being promoted to Captain. General Metzger had mentioned him in dispatches, citing him as a future SS General.

Behind Himmler's desk, on a small ornate table, stood a hand-made SS-Allach tea and coffee service. It had been produced to Himmler's specifications. To him it embodied simple perfection like all things Aryan. He gestured to Schenker, who nodded, and poured two coffees from the plain coffee pot, handing one to Schenker. He admonished himself for allowing the cup to rattle on its saucer in the presence of such beauty and avoided making eye contact with the boy. They were eyes he could swim in.

'No doubt, Captain, you're missing the heat of battle with your comrades,'

Schenker nodded with real conviction. He had a taste for blood now, imagining himself a rabid attack dog of the Reich. Himmler moved away from the window and took his seat. The first thing that struck Schenker was the man's desk. Everything was neat, orderly and arranged almost like a chessboard.

Himmler cleared his throat delicately. 'Our glorious forces will annihilate everything before them. You will, Captain, have your chance to strike a blow for the Reich. Before that, I have a very special operation for you.' Himmler afforded himself a beguiling smile. 'You will prepare yourself for a mission we are developing which requires your particular skills.'

Schenker's heart sank at the prospect of being desk bound and training in a field somewhere until he heard what Himmler actually had to say when suddenly it seemed that this visit was going to be very, very worthwhile. He leaned in closer hanging on his leader's words.

* * *

The couriers travelled as a pair of military attachés hand-picked by Beria himself. They stepped out into the freezing night when every other Muscovite with half a brain was in bed. They were being dispatched from the Kremlin to Tyumen in the Urals on a 4am flight with highly classified documents.

The attaché case containing these documents was locked with a heavy set of hand-cuffs to the wrist of the one who occupied the passenger seat. Both men were armed and the car itself was an armour-plated NKVD Zil. They drove from the Kremlin out onto the main prospeckt in the direction of the airport. The wide lanes were deserted and the first early frost smattered the highway, making the heavy Zil swerve occasionally. The two men didn't speak, fully focused as they were on their mission. In the rear view mirror, the driver could make out the lights of a similar vehicle a hundred yards behind. Obviously the Politburo was taking no chances this morning, he thought. The lights drew closer in the mirror as the car accelerated, over-taking them and racing ahead until its tail lights disappeared into the night.

Both men exchanged a glance - an escort car? The passenger decided to use the radio.

'Is there an escort car with us?'

There was no sound on the other end apart from a faint electronic crackle. The passenger cursed. This car was probably produced near the end of the production month when there were no parts left to use and it was just hammered together. He removed his gun from its holster and let the weapon, with its comforting weight, rest on his lap. The driver, picking up on the other man's unease, accelerated, keen to get to the military airstrip along the empty prospeckt as quickly as he could. The road was completely deserted. The brilliant Spasskaya Red Star glowed over the arabesques of the Kremlin skyline in the rear view mirror. Another light from an approaching motorcycle loomed up and appeared in the side mirrors. The driver noted too late that there was a side-car passenger armed with a machine gun mounted on the front. The pillion fired into the Zil's rear tyres in a short accurate burst. The driver struggled to control the vehicle, twisting the wheel and letting it flow through his fingers as the front tyres tried to compensate. The motorcycle raced ahead and the side-car rider fired directly at the windscreen and front headlights. The first wave of bullets glanced off, then slowly, under sustained fire, the window began to crack.

The motorcycle weaved back and forth in front of the driver who was accelerating to hit it. The side-car rider opened fire into the windscreen and then the Zil's front tyres. The passenger tried the radio again. Nothing but static. The windscreen imploded, throwing chunks of glass onto the men. The passenger fired out at the motorcycle as it weaved and bobbed, the side-car rider no longer firing. The driver saw the other car ahead of it too late. The car that had passed them was stopped in the middle of the highway.

On impact, the two couriers were hurled through the shattered window, glancing off the stationary vehicle, and sliding across the tarmac. The motor cycle swerved back and pulled up alongside the injured driver who was lying prone. The side-car rider fired his machine gun into the man. The passenger tried to rise up and fire his revolver, but was killed by a sustained burst of machine gun fire. The side-car rider climbed out of his vehicle and walked up to the dead passenger. Rolling up his coat sleeve, he removed his hand with a blow from a cleaver.

He brought the attaché case to the other car and the occupants who had been standing by the roadside joined them. They rifled through the case's contents quickly and thoroughly, but didn't find what they were looking for. Then they searched the two dead men. Stuffed down the front of the driver's shirt they found their prize.

The motorcycle bearing only its main rider, the document tucked into his weather-proof coat, turned and tore off into the night. The side-car rider and the two other men opened the boot of the stationary car, dragged the dead couriers over and hoisted them in. After the impact, closing the boot was impossible, so they fashioned a rope with their ties and closed it. They pushed the vehicle over to the side of the road and one of the men produced an incendiary device. He lobbed it into the car. They left, heading away from the airport, leaving the smashed Zil blazing in the Moscow night.

By early morning the lone motorcycle rider, a former White Army Cossack loyal to the late Tsar Nicholas' family, had ensured the documents had arrived safely at the German Embassy. Its Chargé d' Affaires, Tippelskirch, handed over written assurances in return, signed by Von Ribbentrop personally, that an independent Cossackia would be established after Germany had conquered Russia.

Chapter 7

Berlin September 1941

Eva stepped down the steps from Kincaid's privately chartered plane in the early morning hours onto the military airstrip. The sun was rising over Berlin, drenching the city in a deep amber hue. Waiting for them was a black limousine flanked by two motorcycle outriders, engines idling impatiently. Standing at the foot of the steps were two uniformed SS Officers. They saluted in unison, Kincaid returning the gesture. Eva barely nodded, moving closer under his arm.

Neither of them had to display their racial purity papers as they were guests of Dr. Goebbels. Flying out of New York, they had stayed overnight in Paris at Kincaid's private apartment near Montmartre. From Paris to Berlin, the charter had been escorted by German fighter aircraft. Kincaid had used the journey to catch up with paperwork, barely noticing Eva, leaving her to her thoughts. There had been no contact from her family in Poland. She thought of pretty Michaela and Silvie, wondering what had befallen them, then Jonas. She had tried several times to contact his family urging them to leave before the Germans and Russians invaded.

At the back of her mind she knew that she was being hunted down too, the forged letters of transit leading a paper trail back to her. It was a gnawing threat, a continuing fear. Then she'd listen to Kincaid, listen to the hatred in his voice and his sneering toward Eastern Europeans. It steeled her resolve.

She had attended the Nuremburg rallies with him by night. The sky blazed with torches as Hitler ranted from the podium. She had watched in horror as Kincaid screamed 'Seig Heil', whipped into a furore along with thousands of Germans.

If in some way she could stop these men, these maniacs, then she would have to remain dispassionate, focused. She had to be cold, as cold as the night she killed Jurgen Locher, luring him away from a bar and gunning him down, standing over him until he expired, then put another one in him to be certain.

Her covert work had thwarted some catastrophes and saved lives, but this Lenin operation was fast becoming a farce. Chainbridge had received a direct order from Churchill – stop the Germans getting Lenin. He is not to become a propaganda tool - it would shake the Soviet Union if they pulled it off. It would damage Russia's standing in the world and the Allied war effort - don't give Hitler a bargaining chip.

Eva had found communicating back to De Witte harder under Kincaid's constant attention. He was a needy little boy trapped in a fifty-three year old body. During their time together his womanising had slowed down and he was now telling her that he loved her. The cigarette carton messages were still effective. De Witte and Chainbridge could then place contacts in most public places and hotels to collect. More sensitive messages were placed in books and left in book stores fronted by American and British intelligence who would broadcast in code back to London and Washington DC.

Ellen Edelstein preyed on her mind; the solitary figure at the train station as they loaded Jonas' body aboard, she had stood until the train had disappeared. A few of her letters had never elicited a response and were eventually forgotten about.

Now a regular visitor to Berlin, Eva had asked the German underground to locate Ellen. She was found in Berlin, not far from Kincaid's hotel, cleaning the public toilets, a Star of David armband fastened to her old coat. Eva had gone there and found her. Ellen was thinner, her skin pale and in poor condition. Her once luxurious tresses that Eva had marvelled at were now shorn tight to her skull. Ellen had blinked in slow recognition of Eva and shied away from her, hands raised, her eyes lowered.

Eva tried to reassure her and explained quickly that she was here to help her now. The underground operative with her studied the Jewish girl's appearance in horror. They took Ellen quietly out of the train station while her supervisor went on a cigarette break. The supervisor was a heavy-set woman in a warm overcoat, Nazi armband, and plucked eyebrows pencilled in a thin line, giving her a permanent surprised look. In an alleyway, away from prying eyes the women talked, glancing furtively out over their shoulders.

Eva handed Ellen a purse full of dollars, told her to leave with the operative and join the German underground. Ellen slowly regained control of her hysteria and took the cash with a trembling hand. Eva explained to the operative that Ellen was a genius at mathematics

131

and would make a brilliant code-breaker. The operative looked Ellen up and down a few times, deciding what to do. She took off her coat and wrapped it around her tenderly. Eva unpinned her hat and slipped it onto Ellen's head, fixing the pins.

Ellen looked out from under the brim with haunted eyes and whispered, 'Thank you, thank you.' She touched Eva's sleeve. Her once beautiful hands were calloused and raw, and several nails were chipped and broken. Her sunken eyes glittered as if in a fever and she shivered in the operative's coat. Looking around several times he started to guide Ellen away.

Eva watched her one-time friend slip into the shadows of the grey afternoon. As she stepped onto the street, Eva saw more work gangs made up only of old men, women and children, all with crosses on their sleeves. People walked past ignoring them. They were lined up together with armed SS soldiers watching them. Any pause from their labours resulted in a beating with rifle butts.

* * *

The car raced through the streets, the bikes stopping at junctions and halting the traffic, sirens wailing. Kincaid was enjoying this level of attention, his manner relaxed as he made small-talk with their fellow travellers. Eva would translate where the conversation got muddled, three heads turning politely towards her with condescending smiles. Neither of the Gestapo officials present had picked up on her accent. The limousine swept into the Ministry of

Popular Enlightenment and Propaganda where they were met on the steps by Dr. Goebbels.

'Enchanté, Fraulein Molenaar,' he purred, kissing Eva's hand. Then, turning to Kincaid, he greeted him warmly – 'Come, come.' He led them through the stark reception to his office. Coffee was brewing, and sitting asleep in a huge leather chair was Reichsmarschall Goering. His immense bulk filled the chair, his thin sensitive mouth hung loose and he occasionally snorted like a distressed seal. On the other chair was a thin balding man about thirty, who caught his breath when Eva swept in.

'Meet Jack Regan,' said Goebbels as the man rose. Eva noted his appearance – leather jacket, baggy trousers, and badly scuffed climbing boots. He rose to shake Kincaid's hand. 'Great to see ya again, boss,' he grinned.

Kincaid slapped him on the back with a hearty laugh. 'Eva, meet the best cameraman in the world. He's filmed just about everywhere you can think of - The Arctic Circle, Amazon Rainforests and just back from a Reich assignment in North Africa.'

Goering stirred in the chair, the leather squealing under his bulk. He settled again and began to snore.

Kincaid continued. 'Herr Goebbels here has used him for numerous projects and has a trip that might pique his interest.'

'I'm a freelancer, an adventurer, if you will,' chimed in Regan, his eyes never once leaving Eva.

' .. or mercenary,' she replied coldly.

He laughed out loud, but the smile never reached his eyes. It disappeared as quickly as it had appeared.

As an actor prepares for his cue, Goebbels cleared his throat. 'Herr Regan, we have a plan which Herr Kincaid here is going to finance. We plan to create an international sensation.'

He swept his arm majestically to a map of Russia on the far wall. On it were markings showing the German advance, more of a zigzag than smooth line. Eva swallowed hard at the sight of Poland shaded in red behind the line, along with Poland, France, Czechoslovakia and Austria, a red stain across central Europe.

Kincaid explained: 'Lenin's tomb is being transported out to the Ural mountains as soon as our victorious forces near Moscow. I and Reichsführer Himmler have devised a plan with Herr Goering here .... ' Goering was smiling through what seemed to be a pleasant dream, '... to steal Lenin beneath the noses of the Russians. Using a crack commando unit, and a-state-of-the-art airship, we will bring him to German soil. Herr Regan, you will capture the whole thing on film. Naturally with an American financial backer and a famous cameraman, there could be no possibility of a credibility issue. I'll have every cinema from the west to east coast showing it, with syndicated rights for the Far East and the United Kingdom.'

Eva's mind was for a moment shut down ... they were actually going to do it. Kincaid spoke of the footage as if it were a Saturday morning adventure reel.

'And we will display the tomb in a museum when Speer commences the new citadel,' grinned Goebbels.

A pretty blonde secretary came in with coffee, pastries and fresh bread rolls. Amid the groans from the sleeping Goering, they sat, smoked and chatted. Regan, animated, told them how he would film it, jumping up and making a frame using his hands. By the way they talked, Eva thought, you'd think they were going to make Lenin an overnight star.

Chapter 8

Moscow 17th October 1941

The room went silent as the phone beside Joseph Stalin rang. He listened intently to the message from the Workers' Defence Zone, Moscow district. Looking around the table he made deliberate eye contact with Andreyev, Voroshilov, Zhdanov, Kaganovich, Kalinin, Mikoyan, Molotov, Khrushchev, Beria and Shvernik. The Politburo had been summoned in haste and they knew by the look on his face the news was the worst.

Stalin replaced the receiver slowly, his face sunken in disbelief. The Russian revolution had lasted twenty-four years and it was almost over. *We'll be the laughing stock of Europe*, he thought reaching for his pipe. He looked up at the sitting Politburo's faces. 'German panzer tanks have been spotted at the city limits. Let's get Comrade Lenin out of Moscow while we can.'

Below the city, an armoured train sat low on the rails, steam billowing into the frigid night. The locomotive was camouflaged and the carriages were filled with elite NKVD Internal Troops. Ninety soldiers, fully armed and provisioned, led by their political officers and commissars, boarded quickly.

The largest carriage was reserved for 'The Boss', Lenin in his tomb. The interior resembled something between a funeral parlour and a chemist's laboratory. Constructed to survive tank shells, it sat between two heavily armed troop carriages. A custom gantry had been assembled to allow the sarcophagus to glide into it along a runway. Once the embalmers and chemists had boarded, it was then sealed with double-blast doors. The locomotive slipped out of the underground cavern, gradually increasing speed, out beneath suburbs, bursting out into the open five miles past the city limits.

It was seven minutes past midnight.

The remaining troops, who had escorted the coffin returned to the city barricades in readiness for the German troops.

On board, Dr. Zbarsky and his team set to work on the body with a sense of urgency. The journey was going to take at least 24 hours depending on whether or not they encountered enemy forces. Any exposure to air would lead to further deterioration, though the sub-zero Moscow air was of help.

They worked quickly, injecting preservatives and chemicals into the body. Under the artificial light, Lenin looked fragile and hollow, like a dead moth's exoskeleton. Using a mixture of glycerine, potassium acetate and hydrogen peroxide for the skin's dark spots, they brought Lenin back to his former glory.

The new sarcophagus was fixed to an on-board generator keeping it at a temperature of 61 degrees and at a constant humidity. On arrival at the new facility at Tyumen, the body would be immersed into a chemical bath consisting of alcohol, glycerol, distilled water, and quinine. With a special suspension system to allow for the rolling of the train, Lenin almost seemed to smile beneath the glass. He appeared for all the world as if he were a day-tripper going to his favourite health spa, enjoying a nap.

Chapter 9

German Army Group South/ Forward Command – October 1941

The horizon seemed endless, white on white - snow and sky - merging into a blur. Heading this far north, it was impossible to tell if it was night or day, or the position of the sun.

The summer dust and heat had given way to drastic temperature drops and mud, miles of mud. Entire columns had come to a halt in the mire, stretched beyond the reach of the supply lines. The advance was a mirage; points on the horizon never seemed to get closer.

Captain Klaus Brandt looked skyward, watching along with the other units the Luftwaffe supply drop, a week overdue. The weather had been severe, turning the diesel in the vehicles into a gel that lodged in fuel pipes, resulting in engine blocks being lifted out, stripped down and cleaned. Hot food was freezing in billet cans before it could be consumed.

The Chechen sniper who had joined up a month earlier remarked this was a pretty mild late-Autumn for this region.

Canisters fell from the sky gracefully attached to parachutes from the aircraft banking up into safer skies. Under distant Soviet strafing fire, they were retrieved and brought to the mobile hospital tents by half-starved soldiers. Hoping for food and medical supplies, they were bitterly disappointed when the canisters were prised open.

'Christ,' breathed Brandt – pepper, cigarettes and coffee were all they contained – all of them. He allowed a smile to crack along across his drawn features. 'Only Kant could get his dream supply drop,' he mused out loud.

The rest of the unit laughed. Sergeant Erik Kant was the only man Brandt had seen who hardly ate at all. Kant drank coffee of a tar consistency and chain smoked even under heavy fire. If it wasn't for his inclination to act of his own accord, he'd be a model German soldier. Kant gave a lupine grin amid his beard as he stashed his cigarettes into his top pocket.

The canisters were broken open and the parachutes were cut up to be used as extra layers of insulation under uniforms.

A thin army private approached Brandt and saluted. 'The General wishes to talk with you and the Sergeant, Captain, Sir.'

They made their way across a rutted field where the Engineer Corps were trying to get vehicles moving. The air was filled with men cursing and engines over-revving. Exhaust fumes rose up into the frigid air, forming gun-grey clouds. Horses and mules were strapped up to heavy trucks and supply half-tracks, and were being whipped to pull them from the mud. In the white night it made a depressing spectacle.

General Maximilian Fretter-Pico stood with his general staff in his command tent reading dispatches when the news of the supply drop reached him. 'At least we'll get a decent cup of coffee this week,

Gentlemen,' he said dryly.

Four months into Operation Barbarossa, the army was bogged down and his rear units were fighting a cat-and-mouse-war with partisans and the Red Army. Fretter-Pico smiled at one adjutant's comment that 'the front was the safest place to be at the moment.'

He instructed the one unit he could rely on, dispatching horsemen back with wagons to collect urgent supplies. They were travelling back with the light-infantry to Army Group Central. These days any re-supply trip was turning into a suicide mission but, if he was to press on, the army needed fuel, food and medicine and luck with the weather. If not, they would start slaughtering the horses for food as Napoleon had done one hundred and thirty years earlier.

Brandt and Kant entered after being cleared by the sentries. Looking up, Fretter-Pico handed Brandt a de-coded communiqué from Berlin. 'Special operation, Captain,' he intoned before Brandt could speak. 'This order comes from the very highest level. Your unit is now the property of the Propaganda Ministry.'

Fretter-Pico wasn't comfortable with Goebbels and Himmler cherry-picking one of his best units. Three months earlier an operation in Norway hadn't gone to plan and Brandt and his remaining men been outcast to the Russian frontline. They must have really screwed up to be this far away from home. They were very effective soldiers.

Now Goering had put his oar in with some new airship the air force was trying out. What really bothered him was that he was being excluded by the High Command from decisions relating to combat

141

operations in his theatre of war. The SS officer in command was Thor Schenker, Himmler's golden boy, who swept into the tent as if on cue.

To Brandt he was the Aryan race incarnate: immaculate uniform, clean-shaven, hair cropped to a faint white sheen. Even his armband was the deepest red.

He regarded everyone with haughty contempt, even the General. 'Is my unit cleared to leave, General?' His tone was aristocratic, dismissive and superior.

'Captain Brandt's unit is making all necessary preparations even as we speak.......'

'Captain,' smirked Schenker, straight-armed saluting and clicking his heels.

Kant marvelled at the sheen on Schenker's boots. It was almost as if he'd glided above the slush and rut-tracks to get here.

'Captain,' Fretter-Pico returned a soldier's salute without looking up from the reports. Schenker's face turned deep red in fury, his jaw muscles twitching up to his temples. Brandt noted the impetuosity of Schenker's reaction; it could create a problem in the heat of combat. He wondered how cool his head would remain under fire.

Brandt handed the communiqué to Schenker after he'd finished reading it. Schenker snatched it like a child. 'Grid co-ordinates to a landing zone two miles east of the main army group,' he read aloud.

Judging by the expression Brandt observed, Schenker had been expecting this message.

Brandt and seven of his Alpine Korps were to meet a Luftwaffe transport plane at the grid co-ordinates. Joining them was Schenker and, sitting on the far side of the General's tent, a film cameraman from Hollywood named Regan was awaiting instructions.

Fretter-Pico handed the two men the last radio message received and decoded:

- Consignment shipped. Moscow – Tyumen - E.T.A. 00.12. /
90 pieces attached -

'Gentlemen, the clock is ticking. Good luck.'

Brandt didn't like the SS being involved and the presence of an American film cameraman even less. Personally dispatched by Goebbels, Regan had parachuted in two days earlier with his equipment. Once he had been cleared by the General's security, he acted secretively and was very precious about his cameras and film. Tripods, sealed strongboxes and additional equipment had been shipped directly from Goebbels' studios in Berlin.

They can't get food and medical supplies to their fighting men, but can get a cameraman and equipment into deepest Russia. Brandt, shaking his head at the thought, turned to Kant. 'Get Olga. She's coming with us.'

Kant saluted with a smile and left the tent to find her.

Olga, the Chechen sniper, was going to be Brandt's personal insurance policy. During a skirmish with the Russian Army a month earlier, they discovered her in a clearing about to be hanged from a tree. She had killed a local commissar and his men were dealing with her accordingly. A short fire-fight ensued and Brandt's men had cut her down after driving off her attackers. Her kills so far were one-for-one into double figures.

Brandt instructed all units not to wear any purloined Soviet winter clothing as Olga would simply target them. Her almond-shaped brown eyes were almost Asian, her dense black hair fixed in a prim coil. Her scouting skills and ability to remain cool in a fight had made her a talisman for the unit. Added to that, she was an Amazon. Any amorous advances would be met with a mean-looking blade sheathed beneath her sleeve, a useful and effective method of communication as she didn't speak any German. When Sergeant Kant was around, though, she would preen like a feral cat, becoming feminine and friendly. He was the only one allowed near her rifle, camouflaged for winter with white-stained cloth. It looked like a toy in Kant's hands, but appropriate for her petite frame. Kant, as a favour, had modified her weapon to suit German ammunition.

Olga repaid him with a hot tea made of local lichen scraped from tree bark. The brew was indigestible but Kant, being Kant, loved it and requested more. Olga would ladle the concoction with an approving smile into his billet can.

The journey by armoured half-track to the landing strip through the forest was subdued, each soldier caught up with final preparations. The unit, including Olga and Regan, was kitted out with winter wear and provided with extra rations. The unit comprised two engineers - Rudy Hauptmann and Hans Bader - radio operator Herman Schultz, and Alpine Kommandos Uwe Koheller, Will Voight, and Jan Kramer. These were Brandt's best men, battle-hardened like Kant, all experts with weapons, explosives and Arctic survival. Voight and Kramer were also equal to Olga as snipers. Brandt, Schenker and Kant sat with them at the back. Kant stared at Schenker who was trying to adjust his twin-lightning bolt insignia on his tunic. 'Who's the peacock?' he muttered to Brandt.

'Captain Schenker; SS, here to oversee and verify the racial facts of this mission. He answers to Himmler and Goering directly,'

'Must have run out of civilians to torture,' replied Kant. He was lighting up a cigarette from the stub in his mouth.

Schenker looked at him as if he'd found him on the bottom of his boot. Kant held the gaze until Schenker looked away, jaw muscles dancing. Regan kept glancing over at the reinforced boxes containing his equipment bouncing up and down on the half-track's floor. His left leg twitched up and down. In fact Regan never seemed to keep still, even in conversation. Every rut in the ground the half-track found led to groaning and outbursts from him as the equipment became airborne for a few seconds.

The runway had been cleared by engineers and a camouflaged Junkers JU/52 stood waiting with skids fitted to the undercarriage. The engines were running to prevent freezing. The team quickly loaded their equipment onto the aircraft, making a special effort not to hurl Regan's cases to ease his agony.

Once the unit was on board, the plane turned tightly on the cleared snow, accelerating. Taking off at full-throttle, the Junkers climbed steeply up into the low cloud cover, banking westward to meet the train. As in the half-track, no conversation occurred. Regan checked his equipment, all bulky solid 8mm film cameras sealed in waterproof cases. To his relief, nothing had been damaged during the trip. An hour passed and the plane began its decent, banking steeply down, almost pitching into a dive. Looking out of the window Brandt could see only dense forests and snow below. Gradually a huge pre-fabricated building appeared as if sprouted from the ground.

A temporary airstrip had been cleared and a perimeter of anti-aircraft guns towed on trailers surrounded it. Various vehicles moved around and a half-track acted as a temporary radio tower. The unit gave surprised gasps at the size of the building when they stepped out of the aircraft. It was white, the height of the surrounding forest, made of strong canvas fixed on rigid stanchions. It was held firm by ropes attached to piles driven into the ground. At the far end, the fourth wall was missing and inside, sitting low to the ground, was a fully constructed airship.

'Jesus,' gasped Regan.

They all stood looking at it for a moment in awe. Crews were moving along gantries and fuel trucks were filling the four engines either side. Like the tent, the airship was white, mottled in places for camouflage, and was no longer than a hundred feet bow to aft.

'Are we still in Russia?' asked Kant.

'About twenty miles from the Siberian border, Gentlemen and Lady,' said a voice.

They turned to see an Air Force Captain approaching, wrapped in a heavy flight jacket. He was tall, perma-tanned and in another life wouldn't have looked out of place along the Côte d'Azur. To Schenker's ire he gave a casual military salute. 'Welcome. I'm Captain Willhem Rathenow, special flight operations. Beautiful, isn't she, Captain Brandt?' He turned back to look at the airship.

The moorings were pulled taut, keeping the entire ship a few feet above ground. There were no markings to indicate she was German, much to Regan's annoyance. 'How will the audience know it's a Kraut airship?' he moaned aloud. Several engineers heard the outburst and stared at him. Regan was oblivious to the glares.

'Any problems with partisans?' inquired Brandt. Like him, Kant and the unit were looking all around the wall of green, trying to penetrate the shadows.

'No, we've only been here a day and a half. Wolves, yes, and unfortunately we lost a sentry last night to a bear. No sign of the poor fellow, but partisans, no. This country is so vast, Captain,'

They trudged into the tent. It was surprisingly warm. As if it were a tour, Captain Rathenow acted as a guide. 'She took just over 24 hours to assemble. We shipped her in on the Junkers transports outside. The interior is like a beehive, the airframe is treated with fire retardant. The hydrogen mix is contained in small individual cells and stacked into the airframe. Then the whole assembly is bolted together section-by-section. She's an engineering feat.'

Brandt studied it in wonder. 'Does she have a name?'

Rathenow smiled. 'Her name is *The Isolde*.'

Below the airship, just behind the bridge, was an elaborate rig of chains, pulleys and rigging. The tour ended here.

Rathenow knew the next question before it was asked. 'She was able to lift a training 'canoe' U-Boat out of dry dock last week. We carried it twelve miles without any problems. The item we're going to lift won't be as heavy.'

'Yes, but then you didn't have every sailor and dock worker shooting at you either,' said Brandt.

The airship's outer skin looked flimsy. Sustained gunfire was bound to damage it. He knew the troops protecting the carriage would put up a serious fight. The only guarantee so far in this war was that the Russians would fight to the last man.

Rathenow's confidence was unwavering. 'We tested the prototype with small arms fire and machine guns. Nothing short of a field gun will bring it down. The bridge is bulletproof, along with the engine housings and supports. Because of the honeycomb cells, she can fly on as little as fifteen-per-cent effectiveness.'

'How about fighter planes?' inquired Schenker, marvelling at the ship's perfect symmetry.

'There won't be any,' said a voice behind them.

Brandt and Schenker turned to look at a tall white-haired man, resplendent in a fur-lined winter coat. With him, dressed in sable, was possibly the most beautiful woman Brandt had ever seen. He was speaking English with an American accent, the woman translating into German as he spoke.

'We have learned that a decoy train left Moscow the same time with a staggered fighter escort. It's like one big flag saying Lenin's going this way! They even have idiots standing along the line cheering it on.'

Beneath her black sable hat, a few strands of auburn hair had strayed. Her eyes were steel grey and wide-set beneath tidy brows. Her mouth was a bee-stung pout, but not sulky, and her chin inclined toward stubborn. Brandt guessed Nordic or Dutch and observed her eyes taking everything in

Quiet and very intelligent, Brandt sighed inwardly - *rich old men and beautiful women, nothing changes.* Looking at her he almost forgot the war, imminent death, the cold and hunger. A professional soldier all his life, he had never married and, oddly at this moment, felt older than his thirty-three years. Looking at her and her steady gaze, he felt unsure of what to do next.

Eva found herself directing her translation to the German Army Captain with the steel-grey eyes.

'Fighter planes would present a problem,' said Rathenow, 'but I've every faith in your unit, Captain Brandt –'

'– Captain Schenker.' Schenker was again in superiority mode, no doubt for the benefit of the woman. His helmet had been replaced by a jauntily tilted officer's hat. 'This operation is under the Waffen SS jurisdiction. I can assure you, Captain Rathenow, that my unit will perform well in eliminating the security on the train. The Reds will not have time to call for assistance,'

Kant's reaction was subtle. He stiffened slightly, his eyes burning with hatred at Schenker below his helmet's rim. Olga sensed it too and moved alongside him. Brandt was quietly thankful he wasn't in their sights. And knowing Kant, this was going to be Schenker's last trip before an honourable burial in Berlin. The woman in sable's reaction was interesting. Her attitude had shifted up a gear from cool composure to unease at the sight of the SS insignia. Maybe she's not Nordic, possibly Eastern European or British?

'Please, be my guests,' said Rathenow as he encouraged them towards a small outbuilding alongside the hangar. 'The airship will be ready to launch in two hours, so let us eat, talk and prepare our plan. We rendezvous with the train at 19:00 hours.'

The airship's crew offloaded the unit's equipment from the Junkers and carried it onto the airship, with Regan trotting alongside yelling instructions.

They had showered for the first time in weeks in the officers' quarters. Shaving equipment was laid out along with fresh towels, uniforms and underwear. Schenker had gone first, citing seniority, and showered alone. Brandt, Hauptmann, Bader, Schultz, Koheller, Voight and Kramer looked thin as they dried themselves off.

Kant had a scar running across his chest from shrapnel received in France. In the mirrors, their eyes stared out from the hollows of their eye sockets. Without their beards, their faces lost some bulk and appeared more lined and haggard.

'Only the Luftwaffe could get away with this, an almighty airship in the middle of Russia,' quipped Hauptmann, slicking his thinning, wet black hair back with a comb. Turning his head he decided he didn't like it.

Kant was shaving with a cigarette in his mouth, his tongue moving it from left to right as he worked the blade around his face. 'The flyboys always like to think they're gods just because their arses never touch the ground.' The cigarette bobbed.

'Except when they're shot down,' laughed Hauptmann. Hauptmann had now shaved his head, his pate gleaming and red with razor burn. He turned his head left and right in approval at the new look.

'Showers, razors, food, booze - feels more like the last day before the firing squad, Sergeant,' followed Schultz. His big arms patted his freshly-shaven jaw delicately. He was known by the team as 'Der Anker', 'The Anchor'. Capable of lifting a man over his head, he had won several strong man competitions around Munich and caused the Quarter-Master General untold problems in finding a uniform that would fit him. He was the nearest thing Brandt had to a pack mule. Sometimes, looking back over his shoulder on a mountain ascent, all that he could see were equipment and supply cases and a pair of arms sticking out from them.

'It will be in a few hours,' interrupted Bader. 'Let's hope there's more equipment for us other than that idiot's cameras.'

Koheller and Voight remained quiet throughout, occasionally smiling at the banter.

'Let's hope our last meal has generous portions,' remarked Kramer, towelling his craggy features. Kramer, the veteran of the unit, was the last to shave. He had fought Franco's forces in the Spanish Civil War and had been put into Mauthausen concentration camp for it. Prison tattoos covered his chest and arms, and a prison serial number had been branded into his forearm. Brandt had saved him from the gallows, needing an experienced climber for an operation in the Pyrenees. The harder the terrain, the higher the altitude, the better Kramer performed. His entire frame was sinew and bone. Scars and weals embellished it where years of hard mountaineering had taken its toll. He seldom spoke and usually moved around like a ghost.

There was a discreet knock at the door and Olga stepped in. Amid the leers and winks, she disrobed and showered in the furthest cubicle, her knife wedged firmly between her teeth. Never once taking her eyes off the men, she worked the soap through the cable that was her hair.

'Sergeant, your girlfriend's a barbarian....' said Kramer.

'That's my girl,' said Kant with a grin to the mirror.

The table was laid out with exquisite silver service and crystal glasses on a tablecloth of delicate lace. Two large candelabras stood in the middle with candles lit. The company was being attended by Rathenow's personal staff, with Rathenow himself behaving like the captain of a Mediterranean cruise ship, discussing his wines with Schenker. Regan, to his amazement, got a whiskey-sour.

Brandt and his soldiers declined alcohol, requesting strong coffee instead. They glowered at Schenker quaffing down champagne and shouting over the conversation. The food was delicious, prepared by Rathenow's personal chef, Raul, accompanied by French wine from Rathenow's 'cellar'.

Olga and the translator sat side-by-side in warm army woollens and yet appearing feminine. Both had used belts to turn the bulky material into a dress of sorts.

The American, whose name was Kincaid, sat with Regan drinking whiskey and laughing. The coffee was fresh and served from silver pots. Rathenow, aware of his company, kept it coming in large mugs. Brandt and Rathenow pored over the maps once the meal was finished. The map was Russian, the train's journey marked in red pen. There was a dried bloodstain framing a bullet hole in the top fold.

The woman, introduced as Eva, translated the map into German and answered any question that was asked. Out of her sable overcoat, she had a good figure, long legs, and a narrow waist, and couldn't have been more than 25 years old. Brandt was aware of her long fingers tracing the route, elegant like those of a concert pianist. Kant stood back, taking it all in and watching Schenker who was too busy looking at Eva. Kincaid never seemed to be a foot from her at any stage, hovering over them, shouting questions that Eva had already answered.

Brandt called his unit over and the plan was agreed. A sequence of charges would be laid along the track at a point a mile away from their location. Small detonations leading into one large one would force the locomotive to leave the rails without over-turning. The unit would disable the troop carriages and eliminate the security detail.

Regan then discussed his camera angles and wanted to know in what available light he'd be filming in. He was ignored.

Brandt watched the staff clearing the table and looked up at

Rathenow.

'Captain Rathenow, I have a request. As a professional courtesy, I'd like you to put the remaining food onto the transport we arrived in and deliver it to General Fretter-Pico's forces along with any spare medical supplies you have,'

Rathenow looked at Brandt for a long time before he spoke. 'Isn't the German Army able to survive in any habitat, anywhere in the world?'

Brandt didn't break the stare. 'Yes, but we have exceeded our expectations in our advance and have stretched the supply line. The glorious advance to Moscow would be accelerated further with Luftwaffe support.'

Brandt let the sarcasm hang before moving on; the bastard wasn't going to help them. Anywhere else and Brandt would have hit him, and hard.

Eva watched the exchange and was drawn to Brandt's voice and his cold-grey eyes. Not conventionally handsome, he was attractive with a quiet charisma; a natural leader. She glanced quickly up and down almost as a reflex. He was lean, not muscular but strong, with wide calloused hands and no wedding ring.

Unlike the SS officer, he was without conceit yet looked like he was capable of fighting his corner. She had to remind herself he was the enemy who, along with his friends, had half of Europe under the jackboot. As soon as this was over, and if she survived, she planned to discuss the future with Peter. In the presence of this officer she found herself forcing herself to think of him.

Peter was in Helsinki waiting for her, with a berth booked on a ship to New York. She knew the relationship was coming to a crossroads. The choice for Peter was whether to divorce Martha and start anew with her. She was going to use the voyage to discuss it. He was worried about her situation with Kincaid. She was very close to some very powerful and dangerous men. Chainbridge warned her that she could get killed if Kincaid suspected she was a spy. Women had a habit of coming to harm around him. She had been offered a cyanide tablet to use in case of being discovered, but declined, accepting instead a brooch filled with a liquid agent for inducing strokes, just in case Kincaid got rough.

* * *

The airship slipped its moorings, rising gracefully into the weak twilight, ascending to just above tree-height. Keeping this altitude, Rathenow gunned the engines, banking it smoothly away from the pre-fabricated hangar. Within minutes it was in position half a mile from its launch, lying like a shark in the shallows.

Rathenow's crew watched for enemy aircraft from machine gun pods stuck out from the bridge area. The bridge was warm and roomy, with comfortable seats that allowed for some rest. Brandt was amazed how much a meal, a shave and a shower could change a man. Their uniforms were new also, though a little large for their bodies.

'If you're gonna be shown all over the world,' said Kincaid, 'you

155

gotta look your best!' He had remained behind with the stunning girl in black.

Despite his efforts at concentrating on the mission, Brandt's thoughts kept drifting back to her. He told himself to snap out of it. Kramer had confirmed all the equipment was sound, the ropes, harnesses and hardware new. Nothing had been left to chance. Schultz, Koheller and Kant were in position below, out beyond the forest's edge. The explosives were placed along the rail, the timers of Swiss manufacture, water resistant and shock-proof.

Regan was leaning out through one of the doors filming, harnessed to the frame almost horizontal to the terrain below. Another camera was mounted on the bow, taking still photographs for the Propaganda Ministry in Berlin.

The half-track acting as a radio tower linked the airship to Berlin with weather details, especially wind direction. It also acted as an interceptor for any Russian communications in the area. On a secure radio band it kept constant communication to the bridge. After the airship had cleared, the hangar was broken down and loaded onto the transport planes. Within hours, apart from the half-track and the two anti-aircraft batteries hidden in the trees, it was as if the hangar had never been there.

Ten minutes had passed when Schultz's voice crackled over the radio operator's headset. The bridge went silent. 'The Train's coming.'

Brandt opened the bridge door and slid down the rope to the ground below. The hiss of bodies on ropes beside him, and the thump of equipment landing ahead of them, gave him a rush. From the airship's bridge, he had studied the distant Ural Mountains and agreed with Kramer there would be rewarding climbs there. Maybe sometime in the future the Russians would sue for peace and allow Brandt's Alpine Korps to climb for the sheer joy of it. Maybe this mission might be the first step to ending the war.

But first they had to get Lenin.

Chapter 10

Commander Marko Kravchenko knew something was amis when the lights went out. The train lurched once, twice, a third time, and then swung to the right and seemed to grind to a halt. The soldiers in the confined compartment began loading and priming their weapons. Curses and oaths were hissed in the faint light, the smell of sweat and cigarettes mixing with machine oil.

The narrow windows, no wider than eight inches high, cracked under sniper fire. Four men fell at once, blood and brain matter spraying their comrades. The remaining windows shattered and more bodies slumped. Panic spread through the compartment as the doors refused to budge.

Kravchenko roared above the mêlée. 'Stay calm, Comrades, remember your training! Start shooting back. Locate and eliminate those snipers!' He grabbed a radio operator, instructing him to send a mayday.

Sweat poured down the crouching operator's face as he twisted the band dial to no avail. 'No signal,' he whispered. 'The signal's jammed.'

More bodies were crumpling, filling the compartment, restricting any movement. Kravchenko moved back down the carriage stooping below the window height. Above the din of weapons fire he roared instructions to the N.C.O.s. The priority was to get out under covering fire.

Kravchenko began to taste copper in his mouth. Behind him the shooting had stopped, the shouts and screams falling silent as grenades were lobbed into the carriage. This is it, he thought, this is where I die, trapped like a rat.

Soldiers, desperate, surged, pushing him further into the alcove, smothering him. The first grenade flashed and the carriage shook.

Then the rest went off, muffled by the bodies pressing into him. Men screamed, cried out and, like cornered animals, sought escape by any means back into the snipers line of vision. More fell onto the dead, dying and injured, and a pile of bodies was mounting in the middle of the carriage. Muffled explosions outside, followed by the crack of a heavy machine gun, told Kravchenko that the second troop carrier was under attack. The body on top of him fell forward and he realised that he and two others at the alcove on the far side were all that was left of forty-five elite troops. Men were expiring in the choking miasma and the respite was brief. More grenades rolled in and detonated simultaneously, the shock wave throwing him upwards against the ceiling. Stunned, with tears rolling down his eyes, he spotted a rent in the floor. He decided he wasn't going to wait for the next round of grenades. Grabbing two machine guns and a helmet he dived over the mass of bodies down the hole onto the snow below.

He rolled clear of the train carriage, hoping that he hadn't been spotted. Pushing himself slowly backwards through the snow, he surveyed the carnage. Both troop carriages were destroyed. The locomotive had been derailed, making a meandering S-shape along the tracks.

Lenin's carriage was untouched and German soldiers were disconnecting the carriage. Unaware of the carriage being unhitched, some Russian troops had escaped from the second troop carriage. They were firing into the trees in fire-fight desperation. They began to drop one by one as the snipers picked them off.

German soldiers appeared on the roof and began shooting down on them. Kravchenko's mind began to race. Part of him wanted to join his comrades but it was clear that this situation was hopeless. They had been set up and the ambush was flawless. In minutes the entire elite NKVD unit had been wiped out. Slowly he eased into the line of trees, pushing the snow together with his arms in front to cover the trail.

Sitting against a tree stump, he fought the terror that had gripped him. His leg was involuntarily shaking as he checked himself for any injuries. His chest ached from the dive out of the carriage and he was almost totally deaf from the grenades. Blood mixed with snot ran down his face and his eyes swam with double-vision. He fought the wave of nausea that swept him. He took deep draughts of breath, the icy air piercing his lungs.

His head began to clear and he gingerly checked himself for injuries; nothing broken and no serious cuts. Apart from a gash across his upper left hand which he dressed roughly, he was in pretty good shape.

Focus, he thought.

They were in the middle of nowhere, on a secret mission with only a handful of people who knew where they were. Tyumen would only start to become concerned four or five hours from now. He checked the two guns – PPSh-1941Gs - robust, full magazine, intact and not inclined to freezing. His sidearm was fully loaded and, in a sheath strapped to his calf, was a knife his father had made for him although these only marginally improved his odds of getting out of here alive.

Already the temperature was starting to drop. Added to the state of shock he was in, time was running out. The carriage containing Lenin and his embalming team was now disconnected and a German soldier on the roof fired a flare up into the sky. The area was washed in an unearthly red light and Kravchenko pressed himself further against the tree.

The forest overhead shook to the sound of engines revving and in the fading red light the immense shadow of an airship manoeuvring appeared across the snow. It positioned itself directly over the carriage, dancing only slightly in the breeze. The soldiers swarmed over the carriage, fastening harnesses around it. Within minutes the airship gunned its engines and slowly the carriage rose from the rails, groaning into the murky sky.

The soldiers remained standing on the carriage's roof, checking the ropes and harnesses constantly. A lone German was strolling back toward the ship, waving to it as he re-holstered his Luger. It was clear that the soldier was an S.S. officer.

Schenker took his time reaching the rendezvous point. During the ambush he had gone to the locomotive after it had de-railed. Ordering the two engineers down, still dazed from the blasts, he shot them both in the head. They lay slumped beside their engine, their blood mixing with the slush. He had remained out of harm's way as Brandt's Korps had taken out the two carriages.

The little untermensch Olga was somewhere in the trees. The sooner he could see her, the better he would feel. He considered her presence racially unclean for such a noble operation and, if the opportunity arose, he would put a bullet in her.

By the time he was back to Lenin's carriage, it was leaving the ground under the drone of the airship's engines. He was joined by Brandt, Kant, Schultz and Kramer. Olga was walking back toward them. On instinct she kept looking in Kravchenko's general direction but hadn't spotted him.

Snow began to fall lightly on the burning carriages and the dead bodies around them. As soon as the team had assembled, the airship banked towards a clearing. Regan could be seen hanging out of the bridge with a hand-held camera pointing at the carriage. Bader, Hauptmann and Koheller looked up, giving the thumbs-up from its roof. The carriage was swinging slightly, dragging the airship with it.

Rathenow and his crew would have their work cut out if they had to ship it any further than the river. Rope ladders descended and the team climbed aboard. Only Schenker and Brandt remained behind.

'Where were you, Schenker?'

Schenker's jaw clenched. 'Neutralising the enemy.'

'Two defenceless train drivers?' The attack had gone to plan. Had it gone the other way, and his unit been wiped out, it would have been acceptable. That was war but Schenker's actions were cowardly.

Brandt slipped his Mauser pistol out of its holster and pressed it into SS officer's ribs. 'You first, Captain. From now on you will do as I say or I will shoot you and leave you in the tundra.'

'Brandt, believe me, when the High Command hears of a Slav bitch fighting alongside German Soldiers, I can guarantee your remaining days will be in Russia.' He paused then sneered, 'Too bad about that last mission in Norway. I believe it was very, very messy,'

Brandt pushed the pistol deeper into Schenker's gut. It yielded softly. 'You SS officers have no head for heights ... and as for Olga, at least she and I will be fighting men who aren't afraid of a fight – climb up!'

The Tura River was frozen as far as the eye could see and, sitting on the ice, was Kincaid's private Short S26 C flying boat on modified skis. His studio's logo of a bald eagle astride a film reel was emblazoned on the tail. On the nose section was the painting of a girl in a Grecian robe sitting side-saddle on a flagpole. In true cheesecake fashion, her red hair flowed out behind her and her infeasibly long legs seemed to kick joyfully the American flag flowing below her. Emblazoned beneath her in yellow day-glo letters was the flying boat's name – The Liberty Belle. Its engines rotated against the cold, their immense blades cutting the air like scythes. Sitting beside it like toys were five fully fuelled ME 109s acting as fighter escort.

The plan was for it to fly to Helsinki where the sarcophagus would be transferred to a U-Boat waiting among the small islands dotted around the Baltic. A small encampment stood on the edge where the fighter pilots and Kincaid's private operators waited. Standing at the flying-boat's door, Kincaid watched through high-powered binoculars. Below the airship's hull hung the carriage like an injured farm animal. Brandt's team held their positions on the roof.

Kincaid began to smile. 'Sweet Jesus, Eva,' he breathed, 'they have it.'

Multiple explosions echoed above the tree-line where the unit had left charges in the de-railed train. Smoke rose gracefully into the air.

'By the time the Reds realise what's just happened, Lenin will be ensconced in Berlin.' He grinned and began to whistle tunelessly.

From her seat, Eva watched the airship making good time. From the encampment ran a rail that led directly to the flying boat's hold. The carriage would be opened, the technicians removed and Lenin's tomb would be loaded aboard.

The half-track that had acted as the radio jammer appeared through the trees and took up position not far from the temporary rail. It towed the two anti-aircraft guns that had protected the airship hangar, their crews standing on the guns' chassis.

The interior of the flying boat was plush; mahogany, soft leather, polished oak and gold at every turn. Eva sat in a living room area with bedrooms and a bathroom behind it. A liveried steward hovered nearby. She had just finished a meal; fillet of sturgeon, with fresh asparagus and grilled vegetables. This was followed by a Martini, and she lit another expensive French cigarette.

Two of Regan's cameras were set up at either end of the room. A long table with crystal goblets and champagne bottles on ice sat in line between them. On the far wall hung an American flag and on the opposite side, a Swastika. A banner between them read 'Mission accomplished!'

Below the floor was a hold with a compatible generator system for the sarcophagus and quarters for the embalming team. It was dependant on Zbarsky's mind after that and whether or not he would co-operate. Kincaid's and Schenker's view was simple: if he and his embalmers refused to help, they'd be shot.

Eva sipped her Martini, waiting for the moment she would contact Chainbridge and Peter. The pilots started their final check before take-off. Below, the fighter pilots climbed into their cockpits and started preparing for take-off, their engines rising to a screech from a whine.

The flying-boat's radio operator was communicating with Berlin on a secure channel and excited chatter went back and forth.

Looking out, Eva could see the airship filling the sky and manoeuvring to the rail link. It banked slightly, descended, and dropped anchors either side of the rail. Eva started to seek out Brandt among the men slipping down the ropes. She spotted him and found herself watching his every move.

She pushed her hair behind her ear almost as a reflex and chided herself immediately for doing so.

The carriage was placed perfectly onto the rail. She spotted the SS officer hovering near the carriage door, his gun twitching in his gloved hand.

165

He had changed out of combat wear to full SS regalia: black uniform, brown shirt, armband and highly polished boots. Regan slid down from the airship with a pack on his back. From it he quickly assembled a tripod for a camera and mounted one from the pack. Still filming the airship with a hand camera as it inched into position, he shouted instructions to Schenker. Preening himself for film, Schenker stepped back from the door, preparing for Regan to switch cameras. Regan loaded some cameras he had finished with into a basket hung from the airship. He tugged on the line and it was hauled up for shipping on to Berlin. Brandt's team then released the harnesses and the carriage glided down the incline to a stop.

Brandt and his tall lanky sergeant gave a hand signal and, with a roar, the airship rose and banked toward the west, bound for Army Group Central.

Kravchenko worked his way through the forest. There was little to salvage after the German devices had destroyed the carriages. He had walked along both sides of the destruction hoping to find the other two men in his carriage but found only corpses.

He managed to salvage some supplies, ammunition and, by a miracle, vodka, black bread and cold sausage. Undoing his bandaged hand, he poured the alcohol over the wound, winced, and then drank the last few mouthfuls.

His choices were stark. Get Lenin back before the Germans could remove him from Russia or trudge back to Tyumen and report what happened.

Either way he was a dead man.

The airship was easy enough to follow with the carriage weighing it down, but following it on foot wasn't easy. Having been raised in the Urals, Kravchenko knew that the wolves would be drawn to the smell of the dead. As an afterthought he could add them to the firing squad and the Gulag as his options for the future.

He picked his way between the trees, listening for the airship. Occasionally the top-most branches would shake as the carriage was dragged along. It was heading in the direction of the River Tura, which meant he would probably encounter more Germans - yet another way to die, he thought wryly. He kept the vodka bottle as an opportunity to fill it with petrol and use it as a bomb might present itself later.

He began to recover from the shock of the attack and his mind started to focus on what, if anything, he could do. He needed above all else to get hold of a radio. It was still two hours at least before anyone would suspect anything was wrong. The forest began to part and he could hear heavy vehicles roaring, trying to keep the diesel flowing in the dropping temperature. He skirted along the edge and stopped in his tracks.

The flying boat out on the ice seemed to go on forever, the crew moving around like ants with the fighters dwarfed by its bulk. Glinting in the faint light like a prehistoric bird, its engines shook the surrounding air like a gun battery.

Kincaid had stepped down onto the ice and joined the German team. They were relaxed and laughing, drinking coffee laced with strong Irish whiskey. Snow was falling lightly, giving the air a festive feel. Brandt and Kant smoked quietly, talking low and looking around. Olga joined them, wrapping her arms around Kant briefly.

The message from Berlin was, 'Congratulations - keep moving - U-806 is en-route.'

An SS trooper descended from the plane and trotted over to Schenker. He motioned the captain to lean closer and uttered something into his ear. He handed Schenker a message. Schenker straightened slowly and nodded. The trooper trotted back up into the plane.

After reading it, Schenker produced a lighter and lit the paper. It burned to his glove as he lit a cigarette from it, the ashes scattering in the breeze. Separated from its locomotive, the carriage doors were easy to prise open and Kincaid and Schenker strode in.

Dr Zbarsky and his team raised their hands in surrender, blinking in the glare of torches and powerful lights for Regan to film with. Schenker and Kincaid leaned in to look at Lenin. He was intact and showing no signs of damage. Schenker turned to Zbarsky, smiling coldly. 'Good evening, Herr Zbarsky. I trust you had a good flight.' He smiled at his own joke and pointed his idle Luger at the Doctor. 'We have much to discuss.'

Zbarsky just stared ahead.

Bader and Hauptmann watched Lenin's technicians and Zbarsky, Kincaid and Schenker walk toward the flying boat. Instinct warned them that something wasn't quite right. They exchanged glances. Brandt and Kant hadn't been invited to board the plane. Regan had cameras standing idle and he wasn't making any effort to use them.

Schultz was radioing in co-ordinates for their collection by transport, his broad back sitting like a boulder on the ice. He looked up, sensing something too. Years of training and combat operations gave the unit a collective intuition for danger. Bader and Hauptmann started scanning the tree-line along the shore, their fingers resting lightly on their machine gun triggers.

Schultz shouted in frustration, 'Scheisse! The signal is still jammed. That bloody half-track over there – I'm going over to kick their arses!' He trudged toward the half-track, cursing loudly and waving his fist,

'Poor bastards are in for a roasting,' grinned Bader. The unease was growing in his gut, but he was unable to pinpoint it.

Hauptmann tried to smile about it. Schultz's finely honed perfectionism was the butt of endless jokes. Hauptman's eyes kept flicking from Brandt and his sergeant to the tree line, back to his officers and to the river's edge.

Olga stiffened nearby and unslung her rifle, almost sniffing the air for impending doom. The Alpine commandos and the Chechen were now collectively coiled tight like a spring.

Distracted by the activity on the ice, the three crewmen in the cockpit craned their necks, watching the airship's departure. The stewards and attendants blocked the plane's doorway laughing and cheering standing out on the steps.

Regan was trying to get them to pose for a photograph. Kincaid standing at the bottom step was sweeping his arm back toward them.

Eva slipped out of her seat, pretending to get a better view. Smiling sweetly at the crewmen in the cockpit, she stumbled onto the radio operator. He blushed intently under her smile, grabbing her waist and helping her steady her feet.

His headset slipped off his head, and as he swivelled on his chair looking for them, Eva twisted the band-width dial several times in succession, counting 1-2-3. As the radio operator tried to pull himself together, she pushed into him again, giggling as if tipsy. Apologising, she got out of the cockpit and made a good attempt at a blush.

The crewmen smiled and laughed back, saying it was ok with hands raised. Smiles all round and she made her way back to her seat. She smiled coyly at the radio operator as if sharing a private joke. He returned the smile, blushing deeper and without even noticing the radio channel had changed resumed radioing into Berlin on a secure channel.

* * *

The snow was falling heavily in Helsinki. Chainbridge and De Witte sat in the British Embassy on Itäinen Puistotie with the head of Overseas Intelligence.

Eva's reports had been sporadic. The Germans had uncovered a spy and were now tightening the net within the Reich. The underground in Berlin were being hunted down and they could no longer forward Eva's Braille. She had got word to Chainbridge through Kincaid's studios via her agent in London. Kincaid would be leaving for the Baltic within the next week and she was accompanying him. On receipt of this, the two men had arranged to travel to Helsinki, a hazardous trip that had taken over a week aboard a Portuguese merchant ship, avoiding German commercial raiders and U-Boats.

The small basement room was filled with cigarette smoke, the smell of coffee and a faint undertow of sweat. A large tri-band radio receiver was tracking any and all radio signals out of The Soviet Union. The highly experienced radio operator would crane his neck forward at the slightest change in signal.

An unnaturally distorted signal in the Urals area suddenly wavered in quick succession like jabs. It was Eva. The Germans had Lenin.

'What are you going to do, Kincaid?' murmured Chainbridge aloud.

Finland was allied to Germany so it would probably be safer to ship there than overland through Russia. With so many small islands off the Finnish coast, it'd be ideal for a U-Boat or flying boat to slip in unnoticed. Chainbridge knew Kincaid had a private airliner; maybe it was big enough to freight a sarcophagus.

De Witte leaned back in his chair. A sense of dread had come over him, as if being denied sight gave him another sense. He was desperately worried about Eva.

The head of O.S.I. began preparing a coded message to the War Office requesting advice.

'If they get Lenin out of Russia, that's it,' said De Witte.

171

Chainbridge seemed to stare through the walls. 'We could generate disinformation, call it a hoax, a stunt, a gimmick...'

'Kincaid's world-famous; a potential Senator or President. If he pulls this off, he'll be regarded as a bold adventurer who made a fool of the Soviet Union,' retorted De Witte, spinning his cane around his fingers, the only outward sign of the stress he was suffering.

Chainbridge pondered his options. Maps and charts lay strewn across the table. He studied the vast topographical swathe of the Urkraine, Siberia and the Ural mountains. And somewhere within this thousand mile radius was a Polish girl whose chances of getting out alive were diminishing by the minute.

Tyumen was a secret facility and Moscow was denying its existence despite Churchill's offer of military and logistical assistance. The British Embassy here had a small detachment of commandos but if Lenin was now airborne he would be halfway through Russian airspace in three or four hours, not enough time to get men on the ground, not enough time for any kind of preventative action.

De Witte's suggestion was the simplest – tell Stalin directly that Lenin was in German hands, let him and the Politburo figure out what to do, make the communiqué for his-eyes-only.

Chainbridge phoned the embassy desk to notify the ambassador of the plan and request that the commander of the embassies detachment join them below. Turning to the radio operator, he inquired, 'Can you get a position on that interrupted broadcast?'

The carriage was rolled down to the edge of the flying boat's wings. Lenin's sarcophagus was hoisted out and placed carefully onto a trestle on wheels and loaded smoothly into the cargo hold.

Bader's peripheral vision detected movement from the half-track. Eight or nine SS storm-troopers alighted from the back of it. Schultz didn't have time to draw his weapon before he was gunned down and killed.

Brandt and Kant froze for a split second before diving onto the ice. Olga was already returning fire and a storm-trooper crumpled into the snow. Bullets landed around her. In quick succession she eliminated four anti-aircraft personnel before they could target the people on the ice. With tracer fire streaking around her, she stayed put until the gunners stopped moving. She turned her attention back to the SS troopers; dropping onto her chest and making herself as small a target as possible. She coldly dispatched two more in quick succession.

Kincaid was already aboard with Regan, and Schenker and four armed SS soldiers bundled the embalmers into the hold.

The flying boat's engines revved, blowing equipment and Brandt's unit across the ice. Brandt watched Schenker give a cheery wave before closing the aircraft door.

Covering Olga, Kant's MG-34 started blasting, causing the half-track's radio antennae to collapse into it. Kramer stood alongside him, targeting the cab, killing the driver and his passenger. They then concentrated on its front tyres. The half-track's bonnet slumped into the slush with a sigh.

A bullet had penetrated the fuel tank, forcing the remaining storm-troopers out from its protection. Sliding across the ice to Brandt, Bader and Hauptmann pointed toward the carriage as cover. Kramer and Kant half-ran, half-slid, across the ice backwards, shooting. Bader, using Schultz's radio as a make-shift sledge, was already trying to source a bandwidth now that the jamming had stopped.

The flying boat was accelerating down the ice with the fighter aircraft in tow. Two fighters were already airborne ahead of the behemoth. Amid the whistling bullets, Brandt was desperately looking for an escape route as he scrambled back from being blown down the ice toward the carriage. Ordinance whizzed past him, sending up clouds of snow around him. The carriage offered some protection but they could hear one of the ME-109s coming back around for a sortie.

From its open doors Olga, Koheller, Kramer and Voight were giving Kant and Kramer covering fire. The half-track was now ablaze and its ammunition popped and sputtered like fireworks.

Kravchenko couldn't believe his eyes. The SS were shooting at their own troops. He didn't feel any compassion toward the men on the ice. He was impressed though with the speed the small one put the anti-aircraft crews down; one shot, one kill.

He spotted some SS heading out onto the ice out of her line of vision. They were setting up a heavy machine gun with belt-feed bullets. Then he made a decision: the Germans on the ice might be of help to him having been double-crossed.

He lined up his PPSh-1941G, bracing his back against the tree, and opened up with it. The two soldiers writhed under the withering fire, blood pooling across the ice. He surprised two others, shooting them in the back. He stepped toward, the burning half-track slowly, Almost coming face-to-face with another SS trooper, he opened fire from a few feet away.

The scream of a fighter plane beginning its attack run filled the air and an ME-109 swooped past, its on-board cannons blazing. Brandt's unit crouched, shooting upwards. The fighter's bullets clattered off the carriage, scattering the unit. One of them had been hit and wasn't moving.

The fighter banked hard, swinging around for another run, the pilot visible, adjusting his sights.

Kravchenko dodging the ammunition crackling all around him, pulled the dead bodies out and sat into the anti-aircraft gun. Knowing absolutely nothing about it, he managed to crank the barrels upward and point roughly in the direction above the carriage.

Fumbling and squinting through the sights, he found and squeezed the trigger. The ME-109 swept into the hail of bullets, shuddering under their impact. Gracefully it began to pitch upwards, smoke billowing from the engine housing. Moments later gravity took over and the plane descended without the pilot baling out. The dull thud of metal hitting earth and a plume of black smoke marked the plane's end.

The flying boat was now airborne, its immense skis jettisoned onto the ice below. They landed like giant's footsteps. It banked gracefully to the right like an albatross, followed by the swift fighter aircraft protecting it. Lenin was leaving his motherland on the first stage of his journey to Berlin.

Kravchenko stood watching the flying boat gradually shrinking in size. He cut a piece of white cloth from the winter tunic of a dead SS trooper and, wrapping it around the muzzle of his machine gun, he slipped down the bank onto the ice, waving it as a flag.

Brandt and Kant walked out to meet him, Brandt motioning Olga not to shoot.

Kravchenko could feel sniper's eyes on his face, chest and legs. Death would be instant, painless and, at this moment, almost welcome.

They stood facing each other Putting his machine gun down slowly, Kravchenko reached into his tunic and produced an ornate gold cigarette case. He offered it out to the two haggard-looking Germans who accepted two cigarettes and lit up. They then offered him a light.

The erstwhile enemies stood without saying a word. In the space of three hours Kravchenko had lost his unit and his mission at the hands of these men. For their part, the Germans had been cruelly betrayed, now isolated, and they were all thousands of miles away from home. The snowfall was getting heavier, muffling the sound of the burning half-track.

Kant broke the silence. 'What do we do now?'

Kravchenko didn't speak German, but got the gist.

Brandt inhaled the strong tobacco and reached out to shake the Russian's hand. 'Danke,'

Kravechenko just nodded.

Chapter 11

During his time in the Spanish Civil War, Kramer had learned Russian as a Brigade Commander. He translated for Kravchenko as he spoke to Brandt. In three hours every Russian soldier within a hundred mile radius would be descending on this location. Then he'd be hunted down along with Brandt's unit. The Russian High Command would not look kindly on their prize possession being snatched so easily.

Brandt studied the man opposite him. The Russian was unusually tall with tightly cropped red hair, deep-set brown eyes and a few days' stubble. He was in his late-thirties, possibly early forties. The slashes and chevrons on his tattered uniform told him that he was Special Forces – NKVD. He would be formidable if he decided to up and leave and take them on as a guerrilla. He was professional enough to accept that a few hours earlier his unit had been killed and lucky to be alive.

Brandt admired this, the Russian quality of accepting the worst at face value and moving on, his priority now being to stay alive which was Brandt's priority too. His hand had a make-shift bandage over a deep cut and he was suffering from lacerations and small burns to his face. In the half-light he looked like a heavy-weight boxer who'd gone ten rounds with Joe Louis and lost. Brandt, Kant and Bader sat in the carriage with him and Olga. She regarded him with barely disguised contempt. 'Why did you save us?' she asked.

Kravchenko paused. Her accent was Chechen and he noted her eyes blazed with hatred. He had to turn this back to his advantage. He was gambling on the Germans wanting to square the ambush with the SS Captain and the civilian with the flying boat.

'I was tempted, very tempted to let you finish each other off, but I thought the only chance of getting out of here alive is with us working together. To be honest, it all happened so fast I wasn't really thinking, luckily for you,'

Olga's steely glare didn't waver. She didn't trust him. She would watch and wait, then strike. Until Chechnya was free she made it her mission to hunt every Russian down she met and kill them. She recognised Kravchenko's rank and unit. Her mother had been raped in the 30s by the NKVD hunting down local insurgents. During her ordeal the woman had hidden Olga and her sisters under the living room floor. Her father, returning from the market, had beaten the woman in rage and humiliation. The elders of the village convened and the option of stoning her to death for adultery was suggested before Olga's grandfather intervened. He took Olga, her sisters and mother up into the hills to his village and gave them sanctuary. As soon as she was able, Olga had mastered her sharpshooting, learning from her grandfather, spending days in the surrounding forests hunting. She discovered she had a natural talent for taking life. As soon as the opportunity arose she was going to cut the Russian's throat. Looking into her coal-black eyes, Kravchenko knew this also. He gave her the slightest of nods - *try it, you'll regret it.* Her gaze remained steady and accusing.

Brandt felt cut adrift with no role in the army any more as, for all intents and purposes, his unit had ceased to exist. That chicken farmer Himmler's SS could make up any story they wanted. He felt spent. The past few weeks he had witnessed professional soldiers cracking under extreme pressure. He himself had noticed a shake developing in his hand after a mission to take a village a week earlier. It had not gone well and his unit had taken heavy casualties. The Russians had fought bravely even through heavy artillery shelling and JU 87 bombardments. One of his junior officers, Peter Schelling, a former sales clerk from Bremen, had blown his brains out in his quarters to be found by Brandt a few hours later, an empty bottle of vodka lying by his side. It was becoming a common occurrence. Russia was sucking in the German army and grinding it into the snow beneath its heel.

He knew also this situation they were in was payback for what had happened in Norway four months earlier where an SS officer had lost his footing during an ascent, dragging Brandt's unit almost off a cliff-face into the fjord below. Brandt cut the man's rope, saving his comrades and spilling the officer over the side. Himmler hadn't liked that. Within a week they were on the Eastern Front fighting on the frontline.

Brandt stared out through the carriage door. Absent-mindedly he wound his father's wrist watch, his thoughts drifting to home. Every day through his childhood he would cycle out to the veterans' hospital where his father, Michael, lay twisted and broken. A Captain at Verdun, he was a strong physical man, an accomplished rower who had been in a trench heavily shelled by the French Army in April 1917. The sole survivor, he had been buried for days under the mud before being recovered. His two arms had had to be amputated from the elbow and his spine was mangled, yet his desire to survive drove him. As he lay motionless in the sheets, he kept his mind active. He learned to play chess and would call out moves to the other veterans in the ward. Within a year all the men were holding tournaments in their heads playing against each other. Brandt admired his father and came to love his flattened features, a portion of the man who went to war. He admired the way he accepted and adapted to his circumstances while others in the ward had lost their minds or attempted suicide. Despite Brandt missing out on a place in the 1936 Olympic squad, Michael in turn admired his son's stoicism and encouraged him to keep going.

'In the end that's all there is,' he'd say. 'Be like a shark, Nicky. Never stop, ever. If you stop, you sink and drown,'

He had to keep going. His team needed it. They, including the Russian, were now his responsibility. He had to lead them out of this mess. This new situation presented an opportunity for operating with greater latitude. They were, in the words of the Russian, 'walking in dead men's shoes'. He liked him not as an efficient enemy soldier but as a man. There was as simple solution: they had to move quickly to keep Lenin in Russia.

The carriage had sustained heavy damage from the fighter attack. Outside, Uwe Koheller lay dead. Brandt had removed Koheller's dog-tags then had his body carefully placed alongside Schultz away from the SS troopers. Brandt recited the snatches of a prayer he'd remembered over his two fallen comrades. 'When these days are forever past, please bring to all a peace to last. When the sun shines through the rain, thy weary heart shall bear no pain. And when you bring this peace to men, please send us homeward - once again.'

He recalled their first mission in Poland's Tatra Mountains, their actions in the French Alps and their love of climbing above politics, beliefs or war. They were climbers who were conscripted soldiers. A toast of vodka was raised and Kravchenko was invited to toast also. He saluted in Russian. Brandt realised at that point they were a very, very long way from home.

He looked around the carriage. They were all looking at him. He'd have loved to hand the command over to the Russian, but he was injured and exhausted. Brandt sighed; it took a moment to follow through with his thoughts;

'We retrieve the cameras and kill Kincaid and Regan. We have to make this look like it never happened. We'll use Lenin as a guarantee of safe passage to Switzerland. The high command don't want us to exist. We'll oblige them on our terms. I've had enough of this war,'

As Kramer translated Brandt's words, Kravchenko pondered the idea. His thoughts were of home and his family, his young wife Sonja and his four year old son. The damage done to the train meant he could now be listed as dead. Should he be caught, he'd be branded a political traitor and he and his family would be residing in Kolyma before the end of the year. He could be either dead as a hero or dead as a traitor. He smiled wryly to himself that death seemed to be joined to his hip since this afternoon. The German's plan added another option to lying in an unmarked grave somewhere. Tears welled up in his eyes, possibly delayed shock, but more that he would never see little Oleg again.

He nodded in agreement. If he came out of this in one piece, he'd slip into some other Russian unit heading home when the war ended. He vowed to see Oleg and his wife Sonja again, alive.

Kramer, Kant, Olga, Koheller, Bader and Hauptmann sat quietly, letting the idea of deserting and living in a neutral country sink in. This was the first time they had heard their leader, their friend, ever speak like this. They, like him, were sickened at the betrayal. In war life was cheap but this was straightforward treachery. Had Fretter-Pico known? Rathenow? He hadn't turned the airship around once the shooting started. How high up the chain of command did this set-up go?

'I climbed the Eiger before the war; a very difficult climb. We could sit out the war in Berne sipping Kirsch,' mused Kramer aloud, his voice echoing around the carriage. He started to grin at the thought. His creased face resembled a relief map of the moon.

Kant pulled Olga closer. 'I go where this little lady goes.'

Rank and enemy status were forgottten for an instant. They could've been strangers on a train in peacetime striking up a conversation. Then, with a collective grunt, they started preparations for departure.

Hauptmann, Bader and Voight gathered provisions, prepared a

fire and began an inventory of weapons, equipment and, most importantly; ammunition.

The half-track was destroyed with no possibility of its being used ever again. The remaining German bodies were lined up on the river bank and any useful item - knives, pistols, ammunition and warm clothing – removed. There was one odd discovery – none of the SS had dog-tags. Kramer checked under the arm of each corpse for tattoos identifying regiment and blood group. They had none. The fighter pilots' billets yielded more cold food, coffee and chocolate, a full bottle of vodka, some half-eaten bread, cheese and sausage abandoned when the carriage arrived. They were quickly consumed.

Kravchenko declined to eat, allowing his new-found comrades to enjoy his ration. If they were to push out on foot avoiding the Russian Army, they were going to need nutrition. Olga had sourced her lichen for brewing and once the small fire was blazing, some of Kincaid's silver coffee pots were placed on it for the water to boil.

A hurried meal was consumed and the vodka bottle was passed around. Lichen tea followed and those that didn't retch felt the beginnings of being alive again.

Russian and German army maps were examined on the table where the sarcophagus had lain. One of Regan's lamps, jerry-rigged to the on-board generator, cast harsh light and shadows across the page. Sunken cheekbones and eyes worked in deep shadows as the lights began to flicker. The generator was beginning to fail.

Brandt thought the best solution lay with the Luftwaffe. 'We need to get a transport aircraft here and hi-jack it. We need some kind of a ruse.'

'How about a medical consignment retrieved from a skirmish with the Russian army?' Kant suggested,

'They would scramble a whole squadron for a prize like that,' agreed Brandt.

Looking into the distance, Kravchenko calculated that the flying boat would be out of Russian airspace within four hours. Kramer translated this for him. Brandt and Kant knew about the small islands off the coast of Helsinki and the planned transfer to the U-Boat. The flying boat couldn't be shot down because of the precious cargo on board.

Brandt's thoughts suddenly turned to the girl in sable with Kincaid, Eva. She was a witness to what had happened and therefore expendable. He thought of those grey intelligent eyes and felt a stirring across his chest which consumed him for a moment. He'd caught her looking at him a couple of times at least before suddenly finding something else to look at when their eyes met. He smiled for the first time in twenty-four hours and decided he was going to see her again, no matter what. His attention was broken by the sound of wolves howling in the night which sent a primordial chill through everyone.

Schultz's radio was working and Bader was hunched over it, incrementally tuning for a signal. He paused. Inclining his head and practically resting his headset against the radio, he summoned Brandt over to him. 'You're not going to believe this, sir. It's the British Embassy in Helsinki inquiring if we require assistance.'

'How did they find us?' Brandt was suspicious. If The British had their co-ordinates they could alert the Russians.

'It's the only German Army bandwidth signal in the area.'

Brandt still wasn't happy. He got Bader to ask 'How do you know we need assistance?'

There was a pause. Bader's jaw clenched as he repeated the message. 'They've intercepted a coded message from an American flying boat in Russian airspace. Part of the fragment decoded is – Alpine Unit eliminated.'

'How quickly can they get a plane here and turn it around to the Finnish coast?'

* * *

Zbarsky worked silently in the flying boat's hold. The laboratory was state-of-the-art but the available chemicals useless. He was trying to re-think his formulae in his head and instruct his team simultaneously. He made some rough jottings on a page and cross-checked them against the chemicals. Once his decision was made, he tore the jottings up and chewed them when no-one was watching. They were close to the end of the treatments supplied for the train journey and now they had to preserve the body indefinitely. Pinching the bridge of his nose in exhaustion, he pondered his options: not co-operate and be shot in the head as the SS officer had threatened, or do his best.

No point in being a hero both for him or his team.

He blended the preservatives and began to work quickly and thoroughly. They had to hope against hope that keeping Lenin preserved and intact gave their countrymen a reason to get him back. The American's pretty companion was with them translating for them. She looked uneasy and was clearly acting under duress. Oblivious to her discomfort, the SS officer and the American had almost begun a tug-of-war over her.

Zbarsky asked her to instruct that the hold's temperature be set to the sarcophagus' settings immediately. Her accent was Eastern European, which meant either traitor or ally. He'd watch her closely before asking for her help. The fact that she was scared was a good start. The SS officer regarded him with distaste as Kincaid hollered the instruction through the plane's communications systerm. Lights were instructed to be dimmed and only the team remained whilst the body was out of its coffin.

Eva sensed that time was running out, that the net around her was snapping shut. She couldn't disguise her horror at the attack on Brandt's men. As the flying boat pulled away, the small Chechen girl was under heavy fire and Eva had screamed out a warning. She pounded on the glass with tears running down her face. She then looked around to see how she could get the plane back on the ground. Toying with the brooch laden with chemicals, she tried calculate the distance she could cover to immobilise the pilot. The flying boat's engines had catapulted them off the ice and, with the fighter's staying in tight formation, she was out of options.

Her heart ached for the German officer and the pointless ending to his and his comrades' lives. Schenker and Kincaid had roared with laughter at their success and Regan was positioned somewhere aft filming the whole event. The flying boat had radioed Berlin, informing them that they were airborne and that a 'partisan attack' had been repelled during take-off.

Kincaid's personal secretary was being wired to start drafting an account of the events from Kincaid's offices in Burbank, California.

Regan had come back into the cabin area and was hovering. Eva was drying her eyes and trying to light a cigarette at the same time. Regan cranked his wind-proof lighter and the smell of petroleum filled her nostrils.

'Allow me, miss.' He was now almost on top of her, leaning in. Despite working for most of the day in freezing temperatures, a cloying smell of stale sweat came from him. Her cigarette helped kill it off but she found his closeness intimidating. 'Too bad about the mountaineers.' He was now across her, looking out at the fighter plane alongside. He managed a quick glance down at her cleavage. 'According to the member of the master race over there -' Schenker was positioning himself in front of the camera, looking to see if he was equidistant between the flags, and had started on the champagne once he had come up from the hold, his face its usual red rage '- they were racially suspect.'

'Because of Olga?'

'Yup. Better get your face straight, doll. The boss is coming over.'

Kincaid studied Eva for a few moments before he spoke. 'Honey, I find your presence soothing,' he assured her. He took her hand in his and Eva fought the urge to retch. His fatherly demeanour didn't reach his eyes. 'You're very, very special to me and I'm sorry, very sorry, you had to see that ... and, yes, the ambush was shocking but necessary. The SS don't have any experienced mountaineering units, so common soldiers had to be used and alas dispensed with. The newsreels couldn't contain any inferior races, only prime Aryan soldiers.'

He told her he also had information that one of the soldiers was a Communist and former International Brigadist in Spain, then added that a Chechen woman couldn't be seen to be serving with the German Army. Kincaid was searching for a reaction but satisfied in himself that she was teary-eyed more out of fright. Eva summoned her smile from her heels. Trained in emotional mapping by the late Herr Gruber, she struggled to find convincing happy memories to bring to her eyes. Kincaid thankfully never looked past the smile, wishing only to see a pretty adoring face. She gave him that in spades, thinking of De Witte's arms, and oddly and perhaps cruelly, of Brandt's eyes.

Regan, who had filmed for most of his life, knew she was faking and wondered what leverage he'd get with that information.

The table was set in the best crystal and silver. Eva had never seen such opulence. It had to be said these villains loved their neatly-laid tables. Kincaid's fussing over table settings and throwing a tantrum over the cut-crystal gave him a prissy quality. She had been awake for nearly twenty hours and, as she re-did her make-up and changed into the low-cut evening wear Kincaid had bought, she wondered how long it would be before she slept again. She positioned her brooch along the halter-neck.

She brought up her thick auburn hair, pinning it up to reveal a diamond necklace Kincaid had purchased in Amsterdam. Her neck was slender and long, the colour and texture of alabaster, the diamonds sparkling on it. Regaining her composure, she swept out into the dining cabin and into the open boozy leers of Schenker, Regan and Kincaid. All jumped at the chance to seat her, Kincaid winning by a hair's breadth.

Through Regan's lens, Kincaid and Eva sat at one side, Schenker and three of Kincaid's personal staff sitting opposite. Regan lined the film camera up, adjusted the overhead lights and roared, 'Action!'

Through his eyepiece, framed by the flags and just below the banner, the group faced the camera, raising a toast, Kincaid beaming and acknowledging Schenker who bowed modestly. The camera seemed to love them both. Eva's composure had returned and Regan had to hand it to the broad – she could act. She gave furtive doe-eyed glances at Kincaid while Schenker leant across flirting openly. She was going straight to the 'A' list as soon as this documentary was screened worldwide.

Regan panned the camera around the cabin, slowly capturing the flying boat's splendour. The crew from the flight-deck appeared in shot, giving the thumbs-up. Later Regan would film the radio operator informing Berlin of their success, jump-cutting to Lenin's coffin. As they were filming, another unit was preparing to film Goebbels and Himmler receiving the news. Kincaid's team would then splice the film together at Goebbels' private studios. The event was virtually being put together in real-time.

Once the toast was completed, Kincaid and Schenker rose to stand in front of the flags, to applause from around the table. An announcement came over the intercom from the cockpit; they would be out of Russian airspace in two hours. Regan then turned his attention to the laboratory below. He thought about interviewing Zbarsky, maybe taking some of the sensationalism out of it by asking for a scientific slant on preserving Lenin. He hastily scribbled down some notes into a leather-bound notebook purchased from the same shop as his hero Ernest Hemingway. Pausing over the page, the idea slowly sunk into Jack Regan that he was standing on the cusp of history. He was about to become a legend and girls like Eva would flock to him.

* * *

Chainbridge asked Brandt to repeat his statement. The signal out of the Urals was weakening, voices flowing in and out in waves. A few years earlier, Klaus Brandt's dossier had been passed to Chainbridge when he had been collating information on German Army officers. He was assessed to be a very capable soldier, cool headed and inclined to act in the army's, rather than the Nazi party's, interests. He was also a legend in sporting circles, particularly mountaineering and cross country skiing and shooting. An Olympic place should have been guaranteed in 1936, but he never made the

German team. He was now apparently out of political favour and had been left for dead in the middle of Russia. Whatever happened next would be British collaboration with the enemy while German bombs were landing on English cities. The trick was to keep British Intelligence's fingerprints off the whole operation.

'No Russian assistance,' hissed Brandt's voice through the receiver.

De Witte shook his head. 'If it went wrong, Churchill would have some explaining to do. Tell Stalin.'

Chainbridge decided to keep the War Office in the know. Comrade Joe couldn't be contacted anyway. It was rumoured he had fled Moscow. 'Can you retrieve the consignment?' shouted Chainbridge down the microphone in fluent German.

There was a long pause. 'Yes,'

Chainbridge looked at De Witte. 'What have we got in their vicinity?'

'A lot of diplomatic flights have departed Moscow. No-one was expecting the Germans to get this far,'

The Finnish Embassy staff in touch with their counterparts in the beleaguered capital checked UK diplomatic flights. De Witte, confirming the stranded unit's co-ordinates, was also grasping the fact that an NKVD Officer was involved. He started to plan on detaining this individual and getting as much intelligence out of him as possible.

Chainbridge spoke to Churchill's secretary to confirm that Lenin had been snatched. The Foreign Office was running twenty-four hours a day digesting recent news from Singapore about Japanese fleet movements, and now this was another situation for them to juggle.

Churchill had contacted Roosevelt's administration in relation to flights within the USSR. A twenty minute pause on the line interspersed with clicks and hisses followed before the message came through: They had an American Transport still unloading lend-lease equipment for the Russian Army about two hundred miles ahead of German Army Group South in Ukraine. 'Washington doesn't want any US personnel involved,' came the response.

Chainbridge answered in his under-stated way, remembering Eva's photographs of Kincaid's hidden envelope. 'Tell them there's a US national aiding and abetting the German High command by flying Lenin's body out of Russia. According to our information, it's Donald T. Kincaid. This information is solid. We have copies of signed correspondence between him and high ranking Nazi party members. Do they want a diplomatic incident to ensue with The Soviet Union?'

Twenty more tense minutes of hisses and clicks followed before Washington agreed to divert the plane.

'Better tell them to get moving,' said De Witte, speaking fluent German into the radio receiver instructing Brandt to stay put. He had to repeat it twice, stressing that no harm would come to Kravchenko.

The ambassador was uneasy. The embassy was still operating without any Finnish or German interference. No doubt the Finnish Secret Service would be keeping Berlin appraised. Timing was going to be a critical factor; the later Berlin knew about anything the better.

With the lockdown of the German underground, information from inside the Reich was down to a trickle. Chainbridge knew it was going to be down to luck if they could intercept Kincaid. He went out into the freezing night and lit a cigarette. Coughing harshly, he reminded himself he had to cut down. The moon sat low on the horizon, placing the embassy in a ghostly light. Kincaid's private plane was probably out of Russian airspace now.

* * *

Colonel Valery Yvetschenko furrowed his brow, concerned at the lateness of the hour. He was a precise man in every way and the train transporting Lenin was overdue. He rewound his watch, a gift for his fortieth birthday, to ensure it was functioning correctly. Continuous phone and radio messages were being sent to Moscow without any reply, just a constant static.

It was possible, he mused, that Moscow had fallen to the Germans. Since the invasion, communication was at best unreliable and the Russian Army had been driven back to Moscow's suburbs. It was also possible that the train had never left Moscow as radio contact throughout the journey had been intermittent. Tyumen was the fall-back position for the Politburo and Military Command using the Urals as a natural shield.

For months the Soviet industrial and weapons complex had been shipped in secret into Tyumen prior to the invasion. Entire populations of workers had been railed in on the hour every hour ahead of the German advance. Vast catacombs had been constructed beneath the Ural Mountains, more still being mined to accommodate further shipments. Plant and machinery were working round the clock to feed the struggling forces with equipment, ammunition and vehicles. With the River Tura frozen solid, rail links and chartered allied transport planes were the only way into and out of the facility.

If the rail link had been compromised, it was going to be a very long hard winter.

It was ten-past-midnight and the snow was falling with such intensity that a search operation was nigh-on suicidal until morning. He peered into the wall of white falling before him, hoping to make out the shape of the locomotive coming in. His breath was crystallizing in the air, and with every inhalation it felt like tiny needles piercing his throat. He ordered the blast doors on the cavern to close for the night and, stomping up into the radio hut, instructed that messages were to be sent on the hour every hour. All that was coming back from Moscow was white noise.

* * *

Five hours had passed and the sound of aircraft engines filled the air. The dawn was still a few hours away and Brandt's unit and Kravchenko had slept fitfully in the carriage. Olga and Kant, taking first watch, had killed three wolves that got too close. The animals lay on their sides with single bullet wounds to their heads. There were a great many more in the woods howling, watching and waiting for their moment to strike. Packs were feeding on the dead German soldiers, snarling and fighting over the remains. Schultz's body had been pulled up from its shallow grave and dragged into the forest.

The snow had at last stopped and the radio had sparked into life. Brandt's English was poor but he recognised the codeword 'Iskra' as the US Transport banked in to land.

The C-47 Skytrain bounced along the frozen river, overshooting the carriage by a few feet. It turned quickly, blowing plumes of snow in its wake and pulled up alongside. Running below the length of the wing, the team boarded the plane. Before he climbed aboard, Brandt looked at the far bank. At least twenty wolves scattered into the forest from the din of the engines. The pilots gunned the engine and within minutes Brandt, Kant, Olga, Kravchenko, Hauptman, Bader and Voight, lost in their thoughts, were clattering pell-mell across the Russian dawn. Steaming hot coffee was served along with chocolate and emergency rations by a smiling American Navigator.

'Looks like we're all on the same side now!!' he yelled over the din of the engines before heading back to the cockpit. He produced a hip flask and spiked the coffee with bourbon followed by a wink. The two pilots seemed to be flying in frenzy; pitching rather than flying the aircraft through the clouds. Sleep was going to be impossible, though there was one luxury – an on-board latrine. Olga went first to freshen up and was astonished that the taps produced running hot water.

Exhaustion took over and they tried to doze as the plane clattered toward Finland.

* * *

Wrapped in a heavy flight blanket, Eva slept in her seat. Its width allowed her to curl up, the soft leather soothing. Kincaid had wandered off to his room in a drunken stupor, roaring and shouting once the drink had taken hold. Regan never seemed to sleep. Behind her eyelids, Eva thought she could make out his shadow flitting in and out of her dreams. The cabin lights had been dimmed and the Captain informed the passengers that arrival time would be in a few hours. Bad weather had forced the flying boat out by several hundred miles and it was skirting a heavy weather front over the Russian coast.

Eva woke with a start to see Schenker facing her sitting in the seat opposite. He was clearly drunk, red-eyed and blinking through the alcohol. His Luger lay on the table, gleaming under the cabin lights. Eva coiled like a cat, her fingers locating the brooch on her dress. Beneath the blankets folds, she unclasped the brooch and switched to her free left hand. She could hit the jugular as his head was tilted sideways revealing his slim razor-burned neck.

'Frauliein De Witte, Molenaar, I'm a bit confused..'

He leant forward, fingertips touching his nose in concentration.

'I'm not sure what you mean, Captain.' Eva smiled sweetly as if dazzled by his handsome features. He smiled back a saccharine smirk as his drunken mind tried to reach a point.

197

Her hand was free of the blanket and just below the table's edge.

'My headquarters in Berlin detected radio disruption from this plane's cockpit. They've spoken to me about this. The radio operator is one of ours and he tells me you collided with him. What were you doing in the cockpit, Fraulein?'

'Watching the airship, Captain, it was very big and impressive.' Her heartbeat had doubled and her reactions were becoming electric. She glanced up and down the aisle for Regan. He was five seats up with his back to her. He was jotting in his notebook.

She looked back steadily at the S.S. officer. Schenker never seemed to blink, she noticed.

'I made further inquiries from your colleagues in the German underground. They are currently enjoying the hospitality of *my* colleagues.'

Eva's blood ran cold.

'They were very, very helpful. You are Polish, yes?' He smiled at his brilliance, the way he teased her gently. He was getting excited at the thought of breaking her after this journey, once he'd prised her away from that stupid industrialist.

But that pleasure was for later; he had other pleasures in mind after this conversation.

Eva made no reply. She inhaled, slowly preparing to strike. She could almost see Schenker's pulse beating in his neck. His smile seemed to stretch his jaw to breaking point.

'You are a British agent and you're handler is the head of a European spy network.'

'You are mistaken, Captain,' Eva purred 'I'm from the Sudetenland, and I believe my racial papers, signed personally by Herr Goebbels, are in order. Before Donald Kincaid, he was a very dear friend of mine.'

Schenker's composure slipped for a moment.

'Perhaps, Captain, I can explain a little more carefully.' Eva shook the blanket from her shoulders and leaned in. Schenker smiled at the way this clever seduction was unfolding. Eva slipped a leg free and ran her foot along his boot. She shifted her weight forward putting her head close. He could smell faint perfume in her hair and anticipated pulling it closer to him.

'Have you mentioned this to Kincaid? she whispered, letting her lips linger on his earlobe.

'It'll be our little secret Fraulein, if you'll be perhaps ..... a little accommodating with me?'

'My pleasure, my handsome, naughty Captain....'

He felt a faint prick to his neck. He tried to bring his hand up to it, but it wouldn't move. Seconds passed and Schenker's entire body went into seizure. He could see, hear and taste but his body was inert. As consciousness slipped away, he could hear Eva shouting for help.

When he came to he was paralysed. His eyes bulged in terror as air was coming in through his mouth in tiny gasps. He was lying on Kincaid's bed, his head propped up on pillows. His eyes stared at his polished boots at the end of the bed. He couldn't get his feet to move. Outside the room he could hear voices; a male Russian voice and the lilting inflections of Eva translating. Zbarsky was insisting he was not a medical doctor but, after examining the S.S. officer closely, concluded he'd had some seizure or stroke. Schenker was gripped with terror. He wanted to crawl down off the bed and to Eva's feet. Tears flowed down his face and he blinked them away. He was only partially successful. Kincaid and Regan came in and stood over him.

'Too bad,' said Kincaid, staring down at the helpless soldier.

'We could cut the footage, re-shoot with just you,' suggested Regan.

'Died as a result of wounds sustained helping all of us escape,' Kincaid decided.

Sharing a look, they leant over him, pulling the pillows from behind his head.

'A posthumous Iron Cross for you, bud .... '

The last thing Thor Schenker saw was the pillow coming down over his face. His very last thought was that Eva had his Luger.

The ME-109s were at the end of their operational range and banked away from the flying boat, leaving it unescorted over the Gulf of Finland. Behind it lay Russia; its army on the verge of defeat, their cities ablaze and leaderless; a nation on the brink of ruin.

The radio operator had heard that Schenker was dead, from a stroke apparently. He was unsure what to do next. He was just a secret policeman watching Kincaid. It had something to do with the girl, though. The communications between Schenker and Berlin were private and the line between Gestapo and the Waffen S.S. was distinct. You just didn't cross it. He watched the fighters regroup in formation and dive back toward the cursed land. He decided to say nothing about the S.S. Officer for the moment and returned to fine-tuning the bandwidths. In his headphones a message arrived. It was repeated in a loop over several minutes. Looking up at the pilots, he tapped them on the shoulder and when they looked around he wrote on his pad: U-Boat 806. He responded in code that the message had been received and they were awaiting co-ordinates.

* * *

The American transport had ploughed straight through the storm, its engines screaming in protest. It had dived and recovered alarmingly, pitching everyone into the air and clattering them off the airframe.

The pilots and navigator kept pointing to their watches and giving the thumbs up between nosedives with big toothy smiles to the passengers. The Americans had laughed about the team insisting on maps to study as if the answers would jump out of the cartographer's lines.

'If we ever go to war with these guys, we can beat them just by hiding all their maps!' the navigator quipped to the pilots.

The sky ahead was murky but it was alive, lit up with lightning streaks and the clatter of hail-stones. For all they knew they could be ten feet above the ground heading for a mountain. Another bout of turbulence plunged the plane downward before tossing it upward to the hoots and hollers of the pilots. Kravchenko shook his head.

201

These cowboys were actually enjoying this. Tyumen will have found the train by now and he would be labelled a fugitive unless they decided the wolves had dragged his corpse into the forest. He looked at his companions all hanging on for dear life. No-one was making eye-contact because they were focused on the new mission, trained professionals cut loose from their world with no purpose except to chase a millionaire body-snatcher into Finland.

Kravchenko had served in Finland two years earlier fighting at Salla and respected the Finns as resourceful fighters. The Germans on the other hand he had no compassion for, nor had he shown any mercy until today. These Germans could've killed him and he acknowledged a blood debt. As soon as he had Lenin back, he would return with him and help these Germans cross the Swiss border.

Olga felt ill. She held Kant's hand, almost tearing the flesh with her nails. She found herself watching the Russian, the enemy. His facial swellings had gone down, leaving bruising around his eyes. His hand had been cleaned and dressed by the navigator and he was poring over a map with tiny islets around the Gulf of Finland. He tipped her a knowing wink. She just kept staring at him, then through him.

Sunlight burst through the windows as the transport cleared the storm. One side of the cockpit's window had a spider's web of cracks, and the starboard engine sounded in trouble. It had a racking cough and smoke was pouring from the propeller housing. The pilots and navigator whooped for joy, turning around to their passengers to shout in unison, 'Next stop Finland, folks!'

'Great,' muttered Kant, 'we're flying with the bloody Marx Brothers.'

Chapter 12

U-806 broke above the surface. The sunlight glinted off her lines, giving her a menacing aspect. She had been built in Hamburg in a top-secret dock away from the main Kriegsmarine shipyards and, on completion, berthed in Saint-Nazaire away from the main North Atlantic wolf-packs. She had slipped out under the cover of night unnoticed as the French Resistance was focusing its intelligence on the main Atlantic U-Boat fleet.

She now cruised toward the rendezvous point three miles off the fortified Finnish island of Suomenlinna. Remaining above the surface allowed her batteries to recharge and gave the crew a few hours to enjoy the sunlight and fresh air.

A prototype designed for this mission, her forward bulkheads were reinforced and the interior stripped down to the most basic of requirements. The exceptions were the bridge, her torpedo room and the forward hold. These were designed to house and maintain the sarcophagus on its final trip.

Kincaid had paid for U-806's construction in gold bullion and had spared no expense throughout this enterprise, right down to the hand-picked crew. All were seasoned North Atlantic submariners. Her Finnish Captain; Jakko Ahtisaans, knew the surrounding eight islands and sounds like the back of his hand. He had hunted down and sunk three Russian U-Boats during the invasion two years earlier. Though not a supporter of Nazi-ism, he did relish the command of a state-of-the-art German boat and a very generous pay-day if he was successful. Even Kincaid knew that this team for the final leg wasn't expendable.

She was above all sleek and swift, her design spec to cut and run deep rather than stand and fight. As she had been 'chartered' by Kincaid from Bormann and Hitler, the Kriegsmarine was unaware of her operational status. Outside of the Propaganda Ministry and Himmler's staff headquarters no-one knew anything about her. As far as Admiral Doenitz was concerned, she was still on a drawing board in an office somewhere.

From the conning tower Ahtisaans scanned the surrounding sea with high powered binoculars, pipe wedged tightly in the corner of his mouth. A few fishing vessels and transports were visible on the horizon but, apart from them, for miles there wasn't a ship in the vicinity. To the west he spotted a bank of clouds. Probably the remnants of a storm over Russia; it hung menacingly out to the horizon.

Enjoying the taste of tobacco between draughts of fresh air and sea salt, Ahtisaans checked his watch; it was 8.40am. His beard was tobacco stained and his teeth were the colour of the pipes that pumped the water through the vessel. Below, the radio operator had locked onto the flying boat's signal and was guiding it in.

The clear azure sky above thundered as the four 1,400 hp Bristol Hercules engines brought the flying boat down onto the sea, its wake surging back making the U-Boat see-saw momentarily. The fresh provisions would be transferred first, then the delicate operation of transferring the sarcophagus would begin. Ahtisaans nodded to his radio operator to notify Berlin that they had made the rendezvous. He cranked the coding device and began transmitting directly to the Reichschancellry

* * *

In a private dining room below the Reichschancellry, Himmer, Goebbels and Goering raised their champagne glasses in a toast. By sheer luck and perseverance, Vladimir Illich Lenin was in German hands. Kincaid and Regan had done it. This was going to be the big surprise for Hitler, a tribute from the glorious forces fighting in the East. Each man was gambling on this tipping Russia toward capitulation or at the very least a steep ransom.

Intelligence out of Moscow had been compromised which meant the train had been found. The high ranking mole was probably dead or talking at the hands of the NKVD. Somehow Schenker's intelligence about Eva hadn't come to light. Her true identity was still being dredged up from the floor of a torture room of the S.S. Hauptamt.

As it stood, Russia was still playing catch-up.

The first of Regan's sealed cameras had been returned and were being processed for shipment to Hollywood for editing and distribution.

Goebbels outlined the next stage of the mission, in Oslo, where the sarcophagus was to be unveiled in the Nobel Academy. It was to be hailed as Germany's contribution to peace and freeing Europe from the spectre of Bolshevism.

Goebbels had already dispatched Nazi Party journalists and propaganda film units to Norway's capital. As they enjoyed the champagne and canapés, the troika knew that if this worked, the Führer would look favourably on them and they would continue to ride high in the echelons of power.

* * *

Kincaid was shouting instructions all over the flying boat in preparation for the transfer. He was in a foul mood. He hauled Eva by the arm down into the hold and told her to start translating. Regan appeared at his elbow, his perpetual shadow. Zbarsky studied Eva carefully. Between her factual translation she was slipping words in that were out of context with the sentence. He pieced her words together in his head 'We.....need...to...get.....out...... now.' He nodded in understanding. The further they were away from Russia, the harder it was going to be to get back.

Kincaid's attitude toward Eva had altered. He was terse and cold, no longer pandering to her. The endgame was in progress and he was tying up the loose ends. This meant Zbarsky, his technical team, and Eva were now on borrowed time.

Dressed in tweeds, Kincaid's eyes were bleary from travelling and a hangover, and his florid face completed his resemblance to an English country squire. Eva had changed into warm clothing, allowing her to slip Schenker's Luger into the pocket of her heavy overcoat. Its weight gave her comfort. She had used one before and had checked it out in her bathroom. It had a full clip, clear breech and the trigger action was smooth. The last time she'd used one was in Czechoslovakia two years earlier, saving De Witte's life.

Kincaid spun her roughly one too many times and she pulled her arm free of his grip. 'What the hell is wrong with you, Don?' She stood her ground, jutting her jaw outward, staring up into his face.

Wrong-footed by her resistance, Kincaid worked himself up into a fury. He wasn't used to being confronted, least of all by a woman. She rubbed her elbow knowing full well she'd bruise later.

'Your job is to translate. Do it!' He was shaking, running his hands through his hair, the rheumy eyes magnified behind their lenses.

Almost as a reflex he raised his hand to strike her but he stopped in mid-air. The radio operator was shouting down that the sea was becoming too rough to attempt the transfer. In the past hour, the wind had picked up.

Regan had stood by throughout and when Eva looked to him he winked with a sneer spread across his face.

'Christ!' roared Kincaid climbing up the stairwell out of the hold. He could be heard berating the crew above. The U-Boat captain wanted to move closer in-shore to calmer water. Imagine the consequences if the sarcophagus were to fall overboard between the plane and the submarine.

Eva and Zbarsky could hear the flying boat's engines starting up and the floor beneath them start to move. Looking out of the window, they could see the sky and sea beginning to turn grey.

* * *

'Did we land or were we shot down?' inquired Brandt as the American transport skidded to a halt.

The airstrip was a disused farm road that the pilot had been directed to by Chainbridge and De Witte. They were waiting with Captain Charles Fletchmore and four members of his commando unit from the Embassy. Fletchmore's remaining commandos were on the islands around Helsinki looking out for a seaplane the size of a factory.

Brandt and his men descended the steps and were greeted with military salutes. An uneasy pause followed, Brandt and his men wary of armed commandos and vice-versa. Fletchmore's German was fluent and quickly established a professional rapport. Chainbridge and De Witte stayed back and decided on remaining nameless. Fletchmore introduced them as 'Messers Floyd and Jackson, from England.' Brandt knew straightaway they were running the show – British Intelligence? The word *Gestapo* crossed his mind. Maybe Schenker had witnessed Kravchenko's intervention. Maybe this was another deception. Mentally he noted every British commando's position should the shooting start. Kant had unslung his rifle and the remainder of the unit took a small step back.

De Witte sensed the stand-off and stepped forward. He directed a question to Brandt. Noting De Witte was blind, Brandt, as a courtesy stepped roughly into line with De Witte's nose.

'The young lady accompanying Kincaid, Eva Molenaar, how is she?' His tone tried to sound neutral but Brandt picked up on its intensity. He realised that Eva was involved with this man. He felt a jealous tug in his stomach. The man was clearly older, handsome, had a quiet charisma and was blind. He could see the attraction.

'She's alive, but I think she's running on borrowed time. She witnessed everything.'

De Witte nodded solemnly. Part of him was always braced for the worst.

After Eva had returned from Munich two years earlier where she had met the Russian Attaché, De Witte had activated a double-agent in Beria's department, a Cossack of noble blood. He had fed the details of Lenin's transport itinerary into Berlin's intelligence community. These details had eventually led them to Kincaid. Now she was trapped on board his private aircraft with him.

He put his feelings to one side and turned to Kravchenko. He started speaking fluent Russian, making him feel welcome, commending him on his escape.

Chainbridge watched, appraising the Russian as a commando was cleaning and dressing his hand. Could he be persuaded to join them? Being a NKVD Internal Elite officer meant he was hand-picked by Stalin, implying he had some insight to the man. De Witte, Chainbridge and members of British Intelligence had suggested they themselves keep Lenin. Churchill wouldn't hear of it. 'We are not grave robbers, sirs!' he had barked.

The point was moot as Stalin couldn't be found and The Politburo was scattered throughout Russia. With no-one to threaten, Churchill had called the sarcophagus 'a Nazi pig-in-a-poke'.

Brandt sipped the piping-hot beef tea and chewed cold hard bread, sizing up the situation. He made eye contact with Kravchenko who nodded slightly in understanding. He checked his watch. It was 13.00hrs. The flying boat would've been in the Gulf of Finland for over three hours now.

The window was closing to catch Kincaid. Time was also running out for Eva. He was impatient to do something. He looked around to this unit. Olga stayed close to Kant, a heavy blanket wrapped around her small frame, eyeing the American plane in terror.

The commandos and Germans stood smoking, speaking in broken English, using hand gestures for emphasis. They were beginning to relax in each other's company, grateful not to be facing one another in combat.

Fletchmore was tall, soft-spoken and rake-thin to the point his uniform appeared oversized. His eyes were deep-set and brown beneath ginger beetled-brows. A razor-thin mouth was lifted by a full moustache. Brandt assumed he was a Sandhurst graduate, his deep tan suggesting he had been posted in foreign climes. Fletchmore in turn had skimmed Brandt's file and viewed him as an equal.

The problem was three-fold: finding the flying boat, getting close enough to disable it and then to storm it. Then the U-Boat; she wasn't on any intelligence file anywhere, a prototype that had slipped through. No-one knew where she had departed from or where she was heading. The Enigma code had yet to be broken and, until it was, they had no way of tracking her.

One of Fletchmore's men had a large radio strapped to his back. It crackled into life. Fletchmore was over in three strides. The soldier handed him the headset. Fletchmore stared ahead in concentration. It was a single codeword, 'Bootleg'. He handed it back with a curt nod. 'Captains Brandt, Kravchenko, we've found the bugger. She's off the Island of Suomenlinna.'

De Witte's heart jumped at the thought of hearing Eva's voice and the touch of her skin again.

Chainbridge smiled at the stroke of good fortune and turned to the American aircrew. 'Can you get us over there without being spotted?'

The crewmen grinned back. The pilot, popping gum in his mouth, said 'Just point us in the direction you want to go, sir!'

'Great,' mumbled Kant, lighting up one of Kravchenko's cigarettes from his stub. He was beginning to acquire a taste for them along with Olga's lichen tea. He met the eyes of his men. They all had the same look; the look of foot soldiers in a situation beyond their control.

Chainbridge and De Witte couldn't shake the feeling that their luck was about to change, that they were all stepping into the firing line. Brandt and Kramer had briefly discussed defecting to Switzerland with the two men. Neither Chainbridge nor De Witte had made a commitment, merely saying they would pass on the request.

Bader piped up. 'Sarge, what's plan B?'

Kant looked to Brandt for feedback. He got a slight shrug as a response. 'The same as ever, Bader, there isn't one,' Bader re-checked his machine gun, finished his last cigarette and made his way to the plane.

Kramer caught Brandt's attention and summoned him over. 'Captain, I know that man.' He was staring at De Witte. 'I saw him in Barcelona in '37. He was keeping tabs on a fellow comrade in my unit, George Orwell. I remember him because he was blind and travelling as a writer or journalist.'

'Did you catch a name?' Brandt studied De Witte as he headed back to a waiting car. This was getting messy with spies - as if it could get any messier.

'Mr. White I think, Witte maybe,' Kramer replied. 'He haunted The Plaza España.'

'Stay alert, Kramer. We have to make every move count in our favour.' Kramer grinned ruefully and nodded. 'As always, sir,'

Fletchmore strode toward them, and motioning toward his commandos said in a clipped tone, 'We need to pick up some equipment first and rendezvous with my remaining men.'

A disused barn nearby had been requisitioned for equipment and ammunition. Ropes, harnesses and abseiling paraphernalia, along with Finnish Navy dinghies fitted with Seagull outboard engines, were loaded up. The next issue was uniforms. They couldn't have any rank or insignias on display. For the third time in thirty-six hours, Brandt changed uniform; this time it was Finnish army clothing.

Kravechenko's soiled and blood-stained clothes felt cheap and shoddy once he had dressed into the new clothing. His hand was throbbing under the clean dressing and the beef tea had refreshed him. What they all needed badly was sleep, but that wasn't going to happen just yet. Exhaustion meant his reflexes would slow and he was gambling on adrenalin to push him through. They boarded the American transport and within minutes were skimming feet above the choppy waters to the large fortified island, the starboard engine sputtering a smoke trail like a kite's ribbon.

Chainbridge and De Witte headed back to Helsinki, deep in thought in the back of the embassy car.

* * *

U-806's top deck had opened out, revealing a wide yellow maw. Two telescopic cranes mounted at either end of the doors swung out with a metal basket between their arms. The submarine was alongside the flying boat in an isolated cove. The current was strong, making alignment difficult.

The cranes were cranked manually, extending into the opened side of the aircraft. The crew, with the exception of the pilots and radio operator, reached out and guided in the basket. They were being tossed about and balance was near impossible. With a screech of soles on wet metal, some slipped on the floor. The danger was if someone fell into the water they'd be crushed between the vessels or die from hypothermia within minutes. This was the third attempt and the weather was deteriorating. The swell was becoming choppy and grey clouds drew closer, threatening rain.

Kincaid was prowling, shouting, berating and urging the crews to load the coffin. Ahtisaans shouted below to start the engines on a slow rotation as the U-Boat was swinging away from the flying boat and in danger of shearing off its pontoon below the wing.

He couldn't shake the thought that this should've been loaded from a harbour in shallower water. The clown with the camera kept shouting and trying to capture the whole thing on film, panning the camera on a tripod and trying to keep his balance. The U-Boat throbbed below the waterline as her engines began a slow rotation. The helm made incremental adjustments, bringing the bow closer in toward the open hold. With shouts, waves and then a few thumbs-up, the sarcophagus was loaded into the basket. Two U-Boat crewmen crawled over the arms and reached down at the end, fastening the sarcophagus securely.

The process of winding in the arms began. Lenin plummeted briefly before being hoisted upward, to everyone's relief. Crewmen with grappling hooks latched onto the sarcophagus and hauled it in over the open doors. Waves surged over the decks and spilled into the hold as Ahtisaans reversed the U-Boat out from under the flying boat's wing. The whole operation had taken nearly three hours.

Zbarsky and Eva watched the operation from the lounge. They couldn't escape but had discussed in whispers their options. They counted ten of Kincaid's personal staff, excluding the pilots and radio operator. In addition there were four S.S. storm-troopers who were on edge, leaderless after Schenker's death. Two were guarding the open hold entrance, the other two guarding the body stored in the galley freezer. Kincaid had taken charge and they were happy to follow orders.

Whilst they were being well treated, Eva began to notice an atmosphere toward her and Zbarsky's team. The unspoken question was simple – were they going to be allowed to board the U-Boat?

* * *

Olga was sixteen when she had killed her first Russian. Local villagers were being rounded up for deportation to Kazakhstan on one of Stalin's whims. She, her grandfather and his bandits had attacked a NKVD patrol on horseback. The bandits were skilled riflemen and their ponies small and agile, allowing them to turn around tightly. The unsuspecting soldiers had been killed in seconds, unprepared for such an attack. Olga's pony seemed to follow her thoughts, slaloming around rocks and bushes, responding to Olga's heels.

Now on the prow of a dinghy, she was lining up the flying boat's cockpit through her telescopic sight on the side opposite to the U-Boat. She thought back to that day and the movements of her pony. Pressing her legs tighter against the sides, she made herself as taut as possible as the plane loomed closer. It was an immense wall of white metal. The waves were cold as they came over the side. The Commandos with Kant were sitting behind her, Kant aiming his heavy machine gun at the cockpit also.

Once she was in range, she squeezed the trigger. The cockpit window shattered. The form of the pilot slumped forward. She fired again; missing the second pilot with the shot, paused, then caught him with the next one. He spun away before pitching forward off the flight deck. Olga grinned back at Kant, who tipped her a wink.

'Now the fun begins!' he shouted, as faces appeared at the windows below. The flying boat began to drift, its immense blades ticking over slowly. Kant opened fire and the cockpit's framework shattered, sending shards of glass spilling into the sea. The Liberty Belle was now adrift, the U-Boat appearing on the far side of its vast wing.

In the second dinghy, Brandt and Fletchmore were shooting at the aircraft's engine housings. Black smoke began to billow from the cockpit and engines. Brandt watched the U-Boat as the crew loaded the sarcophagus into the hold.

The third dinghy was heading to the U-Boat. The commandos, led by Kravchenko and Bader, began firing at the crew on deck. Men started falling into the water as Ahtisaans reversed the boat clear of the drifting behemoth. The U-Boat's gun was trained on the wildly pitching dinghy and plumes of spray soaked the commandos as it opened fire. Brandt, using hand signals, ordered Olga and Kant's dinghy to the U-Boat to assist Kravchenko.

'Looks like we're taking the flying boat, chaps!' shouted Fletchmore to his commandos. Sea salt covered their features and peppered Fletchmore's moustache as his face creased into a smile.

The wind and spray had given Brandt and Hauptmann the wake-up they needed. They were close to thirty-six hours now without

217

sleep. As the dinghy was steered closer, Brandt and Hauptmann fired grappling hooks and lines from hand-held launchers onto the vast wings.

Once they found purchase, the outboard engine was shut down, and Brandt and Hauptman clambered up quickly hand-over-hand.

Kincaid stared in total disbelief. This is not how it was supposed to end! His pilots lay crumpled on the floor of the cockpit, dead. The instrument panels and joy sticks, rendered useless from machine-gun fire, smouldered and sparked. The radio operator had dived clear into the lounge below but was wounded and bleeding heavily on the polished floor having managed to dispatch a mayday to Berlin. Looking out at the wings through the windows, Kincaid could see the engines on both sides smouldering and leaking fuel.

Shots were ringing out below, echoing around the plane's interior. He dashed to the other side and could see U-806 swinging slowly out into deeper water with the dinghies zipping around it. Crewmen were scrambling below and the two heavy hold doors were closing slowly. This was Kincaid's only chance of escape and it was sailing away from him.

Regan appeared up the gangway from below. He had a deep gash across his face and was clutching a machine gun.

'Where's Zbarsky and the girl?' Kincaid barked. He was looking around, trying to come up with a plan. He needed to get to the U-Boat and the only way now was one of those dinghies.

'Below in the lounge,' Regan said, reaching for a crystal decanter and pouring a generous finger of whiskey which he downed in one.

218

'Get them.'

Regan headed below. Gunfire and ricochets echoed and seemed to be getting closer. The hold where Lenin had been loaded was over-run. Commandos had killed the two S.S. guards and Kincaid's men were pinned down.

Regan appeared with Eva and Zbarsky ahead of him. Eva still had her big coat on and Zbarsky looked visibly shaken from the battle going on below. Kincaid grabbed Eva by the throat, his grip almost causing her to faint. Regan shoved Zbarsky into an aisle seat and pointed the machine gun into his face.

Brandt and Hauptmann vaulted into the shattered cockpit and peered below into the lounge area. The radio operator lay where he had landed, blood pooling around him, slipping in and out of consciousness. They moved cautiously down into the lounge where Kincaid stood with Eva in front of him.

A pistol was pointed to her head and her eyes widened in surprise at the sight of Brandt.

Regan had his gun pointed under Zbarsky's chin, pinning him against the lounge window. He did a double-take at the sight of Brandt and Hauptmann. A loud blast shook the flying boat below followed by silence. Imperceptibly, the floor seemed to shift underfoot. Hauptmann and Brandt exchanged a glance. The flying boat had been hulled and was starting to sink.

'Now no-one is going to do anything stupid,' said Kincaid. He almost seemed to be enjoying himself.

Olga and Kant appeared on the stairs behind him and paused.

Kincaid turned, looking back at them. A smile danced across his features. 'Thought we'd gotten rid of you lot!' His smile cracked into a high-pitched laugh.

Regan had pulled Zbarsky out of the seat and was using him as a shield. Olga raised her rifle and pointed it toward Regan.

'Drop it, bitch!' hissed Kincaid, pressing his pistol closer into Eva's head.

Olga's gaze never left Brandt's. Kant had positioned himself behind Olga where his hands were out of sight. He'd unsheathed a knife and calculated the throwing distance to Kincaid's forehead. Brandt shook his head at Olga. Blood was starting to pour down the side of Eva's face where Kincaid's barrel had broken the skin. Olga hadn't lowered her weapon. Her eyes slipped from Brandt's gaze to the sight at the end of the rifle. Kincaid's temple was in the cross-hairs as he released his grip on Eva's throat,

'Tell them to call back the boats,' he whispered into her ear. Her perfume and terror was beginning to arouse him. It was hypnotic. She croaked out the demand. His grip was like a vice and she was taking breaths of air in gulps.

'No,' replied Brandt coolly.

Eva was losing consciousness. She was going to faint under Kincaid's grip. She slipped a free hand into her pocket, searching for the Luger. Once she found it, she slowly shifted its weight against her hip and pointed the barrel toward Kincaid. Another explosion rocked the flying boat as one of the engines caught fire and the fuel line ignited. Kincaid lost his footing, falling backwards with Eva landing on top of him. She fired the Luger. The bullet tore into Kincaid's thigh and he shrieked. Eva prised his hand away and dragged herself up, clutching the handle of the aisle seat. Kincaid was trying to shoot but the gun had caught on the leg of the opposite seat frame. Eva staggered up, spun and fired again through the coat pocket. Kincaid's head slammed into the floor from the force of the shot to his chest. Olga swung fractionally and fired. Regan slumped behind Zbarsky who skipped sideways, allowing Olga a clear sight. Without hesitation, she fired again. Regan was catapulted into the seat and sat there, head resting on his chest as if asleep.

Eva wiped the blood from her face. Brandt was over to her, holding her arm gently and examing her injury. She looked at him square, her hair falling over one eye and her breathing beginning to slow down. For a moment they just stared, then Brandt pulled her close and kissed her. Eva pulled back blushing.

'Sorry,' Brandt whispered. 'Thirty-six hours without sleep,'

She smiled, returning his gaze below her eyebrows. Brandt noted her eyes were mesmerising. She was incredibly beautiful and his lips were tingling with the kiss. With her heart ringing in her ears she pulled him toward her and returned his kiss.

The flying boat was tilting alarmingly and smoke was filling the room. They neither seemed to notice or care. Kant cleared his throat loud enough the kill the moment. 'Time to go, Captain ...now ... '

Brandt and Eva held each other for a moment longer. They lost their footing as a starboard engine blew, shaking the plane. It separated from the wing housing, sliding elegantly into the ocean.

The lounge was filling up with the smell of aviation fuel and smoke. Hauptmann checked the Radio Operator, Regan and Kincaid. All three were dead.

Kant and Hauptmann moved toward the cockpit helping Zbarsky up and out onto the wing. Brandt and Eva moved next, followed by Olga. Below in the sea, Fletchmore and his commandos waited. They had lost one man and two more were injured. Fletchmore waved with a grin, glad to see the unit appear. The flying boat began to shudder. The hold where Lenin had been loaded was below water and the engines of the behemoth were ablaze.

They were too high to jump into the water and Brandt, Hauptmann and Kant jerry-rigged their lines to lower into the bouncing dinghy below. Eva and Olga were lowered first, Fletchmore gallantly welcoming them. Zbarsky followed, then Brandt held the lines for Hauptmann's and Kant's descent before the flying boat's tail section sheared off into the sea. The front of the flying boat pitched forward into the waves, knocking Brandt off-balance.

Regaining his feet, Brandt slid down the rope onto the dinghy as the commando at the tiller gunned the engine. As he looked back, he watched the vast plane engulfed in flames and slipping down into the sea, leaving a thick acrid cloud of smoke to mark its passing.

Kravchenko watched the Liberty Belle's destruction from the deck of the U-Boat. He was sea-sick on the dinghy and boarded the U-Boat just to get off the thing. They had the conning tower in their sights and two U-Boat crewmen lay injured near it. Kramer had thrown magnetic charges at the hold's doors and one had been successfully blown a few inches off its hinges.

Jakko Ahtisaans was many things, but he was firstly a practical man. The flying boat was gone and another dinghy was heading toward them. With the hold door damaged, he couldn't dive and if he was to hit heavy seas, U-806 would sink like a stone. Ahtisaans signalled to everyone to surrender and stood on the conning tower with his hands raised.

Kravchenko climbed the tower and made a gesture with his fingers to his ear indicating a radio headset. Ahtisaans nodded and directed a British commando to the radio room who managed to get through to Chainbridge who was sitting by a large radio receiver in the farmhouse. He instructed them to proceed to the far side of Suomenlinna, where a deep-water dock was being prepared for the submarine.

The remaining dinghies pulled up, and everyone clambered aboard. The injured submariners were treated on the deck by a commando, one of them later dying from his injuries. The dinghies were raised onto the submarine's deck and secured, acting as gurneys for the medic.

Brandt was sitting against the conning tower when Eva had joined him. The sun had broken through, though it looked like it would squall again. The wind was blowing her hair and, despite the cold, the sun gave off a little heat. The side of her face was bruised but her cut had been attended to. With a splitting headache, she rested her head on his shoulder and dozed, finding the pulse of the engines soothing. Brandt put his arm around her shoulder and pulled her closer; it seemed a most natural thing to do.

The remainder of Brandt's unit sat or lay napping, except Kravchenko and Zbarsky who were in the hold.

Lenin looked well under glass. Zbarsky scanned him with concern, looking for any deterioration. To his relief, the corpse seemed undamaged from the assault. An assistant had been killed during the battle, and Zbarsky wondered if it had all been worth it. Kravchenko had never seen Lenin lying in state, only heard stories about him from his father. His only plan now was to get Lenin to Tyumen. That of course now lay in the hands of British Intelligence.

Eva awoke with a start. The submarine was rounding the island and the deep-sea dock was becoming visible. De Witte would be waiting for her.

She looked up into Brandt's eyes and smiled wryly. 'I lost someone before the war. I'm telling you this as we're probably never going to see each other again, Captain Brandt. I'm really not a very nice girl and my life is very, very complicated,'

Brandt smiled, and kissed her softly, savouring her mouth. 'I know.'

In the afternoon light her hair shimmered. Without make-up she looked much younger. He kissed her again, probably for the last time. He could smell sea salt in her hair.

Chapter 13

Suomenlinna, Finland

Brandt breathed in the evening air, savouring the tang of the sea, burrowing himself deeper into his heavy coat. His fingers sought the cigarette case in the coat's pocket. Before leaving the island, Eva had handed it to Brandt. Inside it, there was a carefully folded piece of paper with an address in the city. The Russian had been moved to Helsinki with the two men; probably for de-briefing, meaning Eva would be there for a while. He read and re-read the piece of paper, committing it to memory before destroying it.

The lights of Helsinki shimmered across the water, a thin yellow line cutting the evening darkness across the sea. The snow had stopped, the cloud cover barely allowing the seven or so hours' daylight to penetrate it, rendering the entire day bleak. He had located the small boat near the dry dock, the oars neatly stowed. Again he looked up and judged the distance from the island to the city where Eva was; it'd take a few hours, but he had to see her. He wound his watch, released the strap and handed it to the man beside him. 'Thank you.'

The fisherman nodded, slipped the watch around his wrist, admiring it in the faint light, then handed Brandt a flask, map, torch and a detailed map.

Brandt pulled on a woollen hat and eased himself into the boat.

The fisherman pushed him out into the tide, gave a swift wave and turned back toward his hut, its lights warm and welcoming in the bitterly cold evening. The boat cut through the water. The sea was as calm as a sheet of glass. Above him occasional pockets of stars appeared in the clouds. Every stroke toward her released the agony of war and, although the end of this journey was uncertain, he felt in his heart it was the right thing to do.

She was waiting, sitting near the *pension's* window, a book resting on her lap, never once doubting he would appear. There he was, crossing the street and looking up at the windows of the building. At the sight of him, she pushed back the curtain and their eyes met like a shock of electricity through the glass. She heard the knock at the door. They stood facing each other for a moment, their gaze locked. He took her hand and closed the door behind her softly. He kissed her. She returned the kiss and a wave of euphoria surged through them. Their fingers and tongues followed a primordial signal from the brain, each responsive and unlocking the code of the other's needs. Within seconds she could feel his urgent heat pressing against her. He reached under her hips, lifting her up onto his waist, forcing her skirt to ride up her thighs. She clamped her legs around him and they walked, stumbled and tripped toward the bedroom.

'Don't make me pregnant,' she whispered in his ear as she nipped the lobe with her teeth. He tilted his head back and laughed. It was a warm laugh and he pressed his face close to her. She could feel his breath on her lips.

'I'll be very careful.' He kissed her deeply again, bending down low and dropping her gently onto the mattress. His hands were experienced and assured. Nothing about Brandt was rushed. He undressed her slowly, planting soft kisses on her exposed flesh and he smiled up at her as she groaned.

'A little more comfortable than the submarine, Eva,'

He pulled away to look at her body. Her breasts were full and sat firm on her rib cage which tapered down to a flat stomach. Her skin was smooth and flawless, delicate and silky to the touch. He planted slow kisses around the rim of her navel and her torso twisted up to his mouth in response. His hands worked gradually up her legs and moved slowly toward her inner thigh, unfastening the suspenders with his free hand. They both moved to a more intense rhythm, their breathing short. 'Now,' she murmured.

* * *

He sat at the edge of the bed, naked, sipping wine. It was Chianti and a good one at that. She lay watching his back in the moonlight. His arms were strong and well shaped like those of a swimmer. There were nicks and whorls around the biceps which Eva recognised as old bullet grazes. His profile was linear, a long nose, not too full mouth and solid faintly scarred chin. It was wrong to compare, but she did. De Witte was uncertain at times with her in bed as if he was trying to avoid thinking of his wife. She finished her glass and rose, extinguishing the cigarette into the empty coffee cup beside the bed. Good wine, fresh coffee and sex. She felt alive.

227

'You have to go. My friend will be returning soon.' It was a lie and he knew it.

Brandt turned to her and smiled. 'I understand.'

'No, you're not supposed to understand, you're supposed to be insanely jealous!' she spat out. She suddenly felt aggrieved. The first green shoot of doubt had appeared in her mind. These past few hours were the best she'd known since Jonas. Brandt leaned in close and kissed her, then burying his face into her hair, inhaled its perfume. He looked into her eyes and she traced the recent scars on his face with a nail. Tears were streaming down her cheeks. She blinked them back, looking away in embarrassment. He kissed her eyelids tenderly; the beard stubble brushing against them.

'Eva, you have your job to do. It's a fact of life at this moment. I *am* jealous of your blind companion and I've been in love with you since I first set eyes on you.' His eyes glittered and his voice had dipped to a husky whisper, the emotion choking the words. His kiss burned deeper than any sensation she had ever encountered before and she became aroused. She slid over and across, clamping her thighs around his hips and sitting on his legs. Her hair fell into his face. 'It is what it is, Eva,' he whispered.

They made love for the last time and, as Eva slept, Brandt pulled back the sheets and looked at her sleeping figure. The moonlight coming in through the bedroom window gave her skin a creamy lustre. His eyes slowly roved over her flesh. Her chest rose and fell quietly and her full mouth was slightly open, revealing her white teeth. She was exquisite to look at, almost ethereal, rolling slightly

228

onto her back and turning her head towards him, sighing gently. She looked so young and pretty, her skin smoothed out in deep repose. His gaze was drawn to a long knife scar across the top of her right hip which had been expertly sewn and healed. She stirred and looked up towards his face. She was smiling up at him. 'What are you looking at, Captain Brandt?'

Brandt bent toward her, smiling back. 'Just framing this moment in my head ... Miss Molenaar .... '

Brushing her hair from her face he kissed her, drawing the sensation out for as long as he could. He pulled the covers over their heads, creating a sanctuary from the night and the creeping dawn.

She woke to find him gone and her cigarette case by the dresser.

* * *

Chainbridge and De Witte stood with Colonel Valery Yvetschenko from Tyumen on the quay as the Russian warship Sovietski Leningrad pulled up alongside U-Boat 806. The deep channel was narrow, allowing little leeway between the vessels as the warship inched its way in. Finnish dockers eyed the vessel uneasily as they moored the ship securely. Armed Russian marines lined the decks with stoney-faced expressions, weapons primed. A group of them descended by rope onto the deck of the submarine and formed a phalanx surrounding the hold. The U-Boat had been repaired and was being dispatched to Plymouth for re-commissioning. She began to power up and the repaired hold doors opened like the petals of a flower.

The Russian warship lowered a series of chains and winches from a gantry, and the men on the U-Boat and the warship secured the sarcophagus. Kincaid had left nothing to chance; the hold had been equipped for a long voyage. Zbarsky had worked around the clock preparing Lenin for repatriation, remaining on board the submarine and sleeping in the Captain's quarters. Slowly, with the creak of chains, shouts and whistles, the sarcophagus was winched up from the hold and within minutes was aboard the warship, secured below decks.

For Kravchenko it had been a difficult stay, being an enemy soldier and a high-ranking NKVD officer on Finnish soil. Once his identity had been established, it was requested by the Russians he be kept away from Brandt and his team and held under house arrest.

Chainbridge and De Witte used this opportunity to interview him at length away from the island in a safe house in Helsinki. They were particularly keen to know all about Stalin, his thought processes and his overall mental stability. They probed him about Yezhov, head of the NKVD, and Shpigellaz, head of foreign intelligence, and their networks. He would shrug nonchalantly between cigarettes, giving only his name, rank and serial number, enjoying the apartment which was clean, comfortable and warm.

The blind one's Russian was perfect and Kravchenko found himself warming to the two scholarly men. The conversations continued for hours to the slow tick of the large clock in the sitting room. Kravchenko's wounds and bruises had healed, his face returning to its normal size, allowing him to shave again.

They asked him directly to work for them, assisting them in the hunt for potential Communist 'sleepers' in the main British universities. A group of four had been eluding the men and they were keen to hunt them down.

Kravchenko's information would, of course, be in exchange for political asylum. Kravchenko declined to work for them, knowing well that by the time the Russian fleet arrived he would be deemed by Stalin as 'politically unreliable' anyway. Stalin was paranoid about Russians being in contact with other nationalities. Working with German soldiers would not be looked on favourably, whatever the outcome. Nevertheless, he decided to go with the devil he knew, repeating only his name, rank and serial number to the men.

Added to that, right now his wife and son would no doubt have been arrested by Beria and be on their way to his headquarters for interrogation. He had to be there with them no matter what.

When Yvetschenko appeared, flanked by armed marines, on the Suomenlinna quayside, his heart sank. He was issued with a new NKVD uniform, without rank he noted. Before ascending the gangplank he said farewell to Brandt's men and Olga. He had given Brandt his ornate cigarette case, making sure Kant was well stocked with more Russian cigarettes.

Olga had merely nodded, not making eye contact, and he returned the gesture.

Zbarsky mounted the warship's gangplank followed by Kravchenko and surrounded by the marines who had disembarked from the U-Boat. The two men both turned briefly and waved goodbye. Brandt, Kramer, Kant, Bader and Hauptman gave a soldier's salute in return, dressed now in civilian clothes.

The Sovietski Leningrad slipped back into the dawn light and departed Suomenlinna. Just south of the island, a flotilla of Russian warships waited for the ship with its precious cargo aboard. Once it joined the convoy, the armada set sail for the motherland of Russia. They were going to sail close to the Finnish and Swedish coastline and back around to Murmansk, running the German U-Boat gauntlet of the North Atlantic.

Kravchenko stared out from the deck as the surrounding islands slipped past, his thoughts never far from Sondra and Oleg. Maybe when this war was over, when the years of bloodshed had passed, he'd return here with them.

Chainbridge got word to the American Embassy in London that Donald T Kincaid's private flying boat had gone missing during a storm over Finland. Rescue efforts were being hampered by severe weather conditions and hopes were fading for survivors.

Yvetschenko lit a cigarette and offered one to Chainbridge. 'This unfortunate incident never occurred, Mr Chainbridge.'

'Of course, Colonel,' replied Chainbridge, exhaling slowly. Studying the Colonel, Chainbridge guessed he was more or less his opposite in the NKVD, a fellow spymaster.

'Did any of the film footage get to Berlin?' Yvetschenko inquired. He hadn't decided Kravchenko's fate yet. No doubt Stalin would want to talk to him personally. He had wanted Brandt's unit handed over to him for execution, but Chainbridge and De Witte wouldn't countenance it.

Chainbridge pulled his coats lapels closer across his chest in the cold. 'Some footage may have got through, Comrade Yvetschenko, though who would believe it?'

The flying boat had sunk quickly, the water several fathoms deep in the area it went down, but there was always the possibility of one of Regan's cameras being washed ashore. However, for now, the mission had been accomplished.

'Colonel, I have a personal favour.' Chainbridge extinguished his cigarette with his heel. 'Spare the dockworkers. This isn't their war.'

The Russian Colonel showed no expression as he stepped forward and raised his left arm straight. At this signal, the marines aboard the warship lowered their weapons and returned below decks.

'Thank you,' smiled Chainbridge. Yvetschenko merely grunted as he skulked away, burying his head deep into his coats lapels. He ascended the gangplank without looking back.

Brandt watched Eva and De Witte standing together, looking for a sign. Weighing heavily in his tunic's pocket was a letter to her. It had taken hours to write and now he felt there was no point to it.

For a week he had remained in the farm house on the island after seeing her for the most part existing in a vacuum. There she stood at the quayside and his heart jumped at the sight of her. She made eye-contact often but didn't give any indication of her true emotions, fussing and minding De Witte. Brandt observed she was making a

233

meal of it and laughed to himself for being so foolish. He was an enemy soldier displaced on foreign soil and was at the mercy of these men, Jackson and Floyd. Nevertheless, any time she looked up it was always toward him.

He stepped out of her eye line and, when she looked up to find him missing, she searched for him. When they made eye contact again, he tipped her a wink. She blushed and got flustered, patting down one of De Witte's coat lapels with added intensity.

His thoughts were broken when Chainbridge and Fletchmore came up to him and handed him a large manila envelope. Inside were letters of transit prepared by the British Embassy for Switzerland. False passports requiring new photographs, currency and rations were handed to him also.

'Captain Brandt, you've made an awful lot of enemies. Norway aside, if the High Command finds out you and your men survived, they'll hunt you down,'

'Very few are mountaineers,' smiled Brandt. He worried about his mother in Düsseldorf who would now have received a letter telling her he was dead. His men too had families in Germany and they had no idea what their fate would be. 'How are we going to get there?' he inquired.

Chainbridge nodded toward the pilots of the American Transport. The pilots and navigator were sitting in an army Jeep, the engine idling like a hot-rod.

'Jesus,' muttered Kant.

Brandt shook the hands of Chainbridge and De Witte.

Chainbridge gripped his hand. 'Captain Brandt, think of this as a rest and recreation break for you and your team. We may have to call upon you and your team's services again.'

Brandt was amused by the idea of being a soldier of fortune, but for now had no plans.

He came to Eva. 'Fraulein.' He held her hand gently and she didn't pull it away.

'Au revoir, Captain' she smiled. 'I'm leaving for New York tonight.'

He couldn't tear his eyes away from her mouth.

'Au revoir, Eva,' he replied. 'Have a safe voyage.'

Eva stood on the deck, leaning against the rail, deep in thought. She felt drained although the adrenalin of the past two months still pumped fast through her veins. The boat was a fishing smack hired by Chainbridge and De Witte who were both dozing in the bridge under the leisurely pace of the journey. From Helsinki, she and De Witte were sailing to New York in a ship sporting the Finnish flag, thus improving their chances against the German wolf packs of the Atlantic Ocean. She bundled herself deeper into her great coat, trying to control her billowing hair as she stared into the ship's wake.

She reached for her cigarette case and lit up a cigarette with her back to the breeze. The engines of an aeroplane made her look up. It was the American transporter banking upward, one of the engines still cracking and popping as it revved.

As it ascended, she thought of Captain Brandt and a certainty welled up in her that she was going to meet him again. It was a delicious, uncertain sensation.

Made in the USA
Charleston, SC
02 March 2012